The Space Between Our Hearts

Praise for Hannah Stone's
The Space Between Our Hearts

A moving and deep story about love, friendship, and most of all, finding your place in this world. Hannah Stone weaves together an emotional debut bursting with beautiful prose and unforgettable characters.

— Jennie Wexler, author of *Where It All Lands*

What an achingly beautiful story! In *The Space Between Our Hearts*, not only does author Hannah Stone give us a romantic summer at the beach, but she's done it with a deeply flawed and immensely likable heroine you can't help but root for. Fans of *Eleanor and Park*, lovers of contemporary YA, and those looking for a wrong-side-of-the-tracks romance with a found family thrown in will eat this one up. And well they should!

— Shannon Dittemore award-winning author of *Winter, White and Wicked*

The Space Between Our Hearts

Hannah Stone

ISBN: 979-8-9944152-0-7

Cover art by Polina Bakalina

Jo and Liz

I will always hold the door open for you,
or stretch a sweater and become a door myself.

1

Everything I own is inside this backpack. And when I shove my hand in, searching by feel for the skirt that hugs my curves like a NASCAR driver, I discover that everything is covered in goo.

I wipe the slime across my thigh.

I don't have time for this.

I have exactly ten minutes until my interview starts and this cannot be happening. But here it is, the skirt I bought specifically for today, ruined. When I fling it to the floor, a lidless body butter container rolls out from the folds of fabric, making a smudge across the marble tiles.

There's a list of places where my life has taken a horrible turn; a gas station, the middle school sports equipment shed, and now a hotel lobby bathroom. I shouldn't be surprised by this, but I am. Having the bus pull into the station at Tinlee

Bay two hours late because of a construction delay already had me on edge, but what am I supposed to do now?

Pinching the bridge of my nose, I attempt a breathing exercise I learned in group therapy, but I don't have time to calm down, I have seven minutes left.

Life has always dealt me an unfair hand; it has been happening on repeat since I was born. My one-way ticket to California was supposed to be the cure for all the bad luck that clings to me like a skin I can never shed. Aging out of the foster system isn't exactly a rabbit-foot key chain I can hold on to.

I kick the globby skirt at my feet before shoving it back into the depths of my backpack—because I have no other option. Yanking the gold faucet handle all the way hot, I scrub my face, hating the fact I'm about to go to a job interview in my pajamas. Technically these three-dollar leggings with fabric pilling between my thighs, and my faded Smokey the Bear T-shirt that I cut the neck off of are not my pajamas, but they might as well be. I've been wearing them since I woke up and left without saying goodbye. That was two days ago. But I can't worry over slime-coated failures and pajama-wearing interviews. I have five minutes left.

In the lobby of the B Hive, I allow myself half a minute to gawk. Everything is white with gold accents. Two leather couches are angled in front of a massive stone fireplace and they look like you would need help getting out of them if you decided to sit. A few accent chairs are strategically scattered throughout the space as well, alternating between bold floral patterns or deep velvet perfection. I fight the urge to pull out the page I ripped from a magazine and hold it in the perfect alignment until the frayed edges of the glossy paper blend with reality. For the past year, I've kept pictures of this hotel in my pocket, imagining myself in this very spot. Despite my rocky start, I am proud of myself for standing here and not just dreaming about it.

I could have stayed in Montana, found a place to live, and kept working for the Clean Sweep full-time instead of after school or on the weekends. But there is nothing for me in Montana; there never has been.

"Can I help you?" The voice from the other side of reception makes me jump.

Offering my best smile, I say, "I have an interview for the housekeeping position."

The woman slides her eyes across my outfit before looking back at my face and I curve my lips so tight they almost crack. Extending her arm out, she points down a hall at the side of reception. "Last door on your right." As I round the desk, she says something that sounds like *good luck.*

The nameplate next to the last door on the right reads *Beverly* in scripted gold, and when I read it for a second time, I almost throw up. Did I misunderstand? This is the only hallway and there are only two doors, so the odds of me getting it wrong are slim. The other door has a keypad attached to the doorknob and *staff bathroom* is written in bold white letters on the black door.

I should be interviewing with the head of housekeeping,

not Beverly, owner, and Chief Aesthetic Operator—her words—of the B Hive. She built this business from nothing into the hotel voted California's Choice five years running, and I'll be face-to-face with her dressed like I slept in my clothes. Which I did, on the bus.

Why is this my life? In all my eighteen years, why has nothing ever gone right?

I'm about to knock when I remember my backpack. My entire life is inside this bag; leaving it, even for a second, makes my heart race. But I shouldn't have it with me either. At the end of the hall, two urns erupting with pampas grass flank a large window. Tucking my faded yellow backpack behind the plant, I attempt to fan the spears of feathered grass wider to keep it covered. I don't know if it made a difference, so I whisper, *"Please be here when I get back,"* under my breath.

The door opens immediately after my knuckles rap and Beverly Lambert, a woman who deserves her own HGTV show, stands on the other side. My throat is so dry I can't even say hello.

Beverly's expression is hard to decipher as she glances at her watch. "Punctual."

She blinks at me several times without her eyes sliding down to the wrinkled face of Smokey, which must take a herculean effort on her part. She practically glides back to her desk in her black slacks, black ribbed short-sleeve turtleneck with a thin gold belt cinching her equally thin waist. Her blond hair skims shoulders that I imagine never slouch.

Mine are hunched forward from years of trying to take up as little space as possible. Beverly is sleek and professional and I'm a pile of dirty laundry.

I try not to ever think about who is to blame for my shapely frame—him or her. Most people refer to their parents as mom and dad, but I never knew either one so all they get are pronouns, which seems more than generous.

Beverly gestures to the door and I close it before taking a seat. Hanging on the wall behind her is an oversized photograph of a sunset illuminating three people walking on the beach. In it, Beverly holds hands with a small boy who holds hands with her husband. From my hours of internet research, I know this picture is not recent, because her son isn't that much older than I am. Beverly's family in high-resolution pixels is flawless, like everything else I've ever seen or read of her life. Again, the exact opposite of mine.

I breathe in, trying to relax the space between my eyes while forcing myself to uncurl my shoulders. I can do this. I need to take the nothing of my life and make it something, I need to nail this interview and get the job. And if there's one thing I can do, it's clean up the mess other people leave behind.

Beverly slips on a pair of black glasses, checking the paper on her desk. "Rindy. That's not a common name, is it?"

At that, I sit up a little straighter. I've been waiting for this, and it sends a shiver down my spine. As I watched Montana bleed into the background out the Greyhound window, my body hummed with anticipation for this very moment. Growing up, in-between Nowhere and Not-Much, everyone knew everyone, and all I've ever been is the girl who was found. It never helped that every few years my story made the local news cycle all over again and I could never escape my past.

No one knows me here, and while I can't erase history, it doesn't mean I have to tell the truth.

Keeping my brown eyes locked on her blue ones, I lie. "Old family name."

And who knows, maybe it is. The night manager at a gas station found me in a cardboard box shoved between two pumps. I was wrapped in a blanket, a scrap of paper tucked underneath me. *Her name is Rindy* was written in slanted blue penmanship.

I used to wish it was a clue I was meant to follow. But it wasn't. It was just a name. Beverly nods, unaware of my lie, and for the first time today, my heart pumps with relief. Something is finally going exactly the way I planned.

2

Homogenous.

The word sounds like sour milk.

After I calmed down, I sailed through the interview, answering every question with solid answers. I even made Beverly smile. A wave of confidence had swept over me as Beverly held the door open after the interview ended and we exchanged goodbyes. But then she'd placed her free hand on my arm and said, "Here at the B Hive I've worked hard to cultivate a certain standard." She'd paused, releasing my arm, and taking off her glasses before landing the punch, "A homogenous standard." Her eyes had finally left mine, darting to my shirt and threadbare leggings before coming back up to my exhausted, red-rimmed eyes. After that, any ounce of confidence I managed to collect was gone.

I was seven when my social worker brought me to yet

another foster family. The husband opened the door, and a few steps behind him stood his wife, a child peeking out from behind her leg. The mom and daughter shared the exact same shade of strawberry blonde hair. As my social worker talked, I scanned the living room, finding the walls covered in photos of the husband and wife. Their wedding. A pumpkin patch. A tropical beach. A snow-filled yard in front of an A-frame cabin. It was only the two of them. No swollen stomach, no proud hospital smile and screaming newborn, nothing.

That girl looked like a photocopy of the woman but when my social worker said, "Thanks for taking another one on short notice," I realized the shy redhead was also in the system. I didn't resemble anyone in this family with my brown hair, brown eyes, and skin that tans at the mention of the sun. Hard to blend in when I'm the one who stuck out. Today felt the same.

Beverly said she had one more interview and she'd be in touch tomorrow morning. It's going to be a long wait. Kicking a rock, I lift my eyes from the horseshoe driveway in front of the hotel as I shift my backpack further up my shoulders. The B Hive is perched on top of a hill overlooking the Pacific Ocean, and as I exit the parking lot, starting my descent into town, I finally take in the breathtaking view.

How anyone could get used to a view like this, and carry on with their day as if it's not the most spectacular thing they've ever encountered, is beyond me. The ocean is endless, and shimmering, and I can't believe I am going to live here. A nagging voice that sounds a lot like Beverly saying *homogenous* curls at the back of my head. *We'll see about that.* It circles once, twice, mimicking a dog making itself comfortable for a long nap, and I don't have the energy to stop it.

Moving to Tinlee Bay is everything I've waited and saved for. But what if I can't reinvent myself? What if I'm stuck as the same person I've always been? That creates an ache in my chest as sudden and painful as slamming a finger in a car door.

Unwanted. Abandoned. Overweight.

Round Rindy was a nickname that started on the elementary playground, and it became a cockroach of a nickname—no matter what I did, it never died.

Beverly never said words like that, but she didn't have to. The message from the flash in her eyes, when she said homogenous, was loud and clear. I do not fit her standard.

The end of the interview haunts me until I'm finally walking through the heart of Tinlee Bay. Lambert Avenue is a long luscious main street made up of unique boutiques and art galleries with an Asian market smack in the middle. Gigantic flowering baskets hang from Narnia-style streetlamps, occasionally dropping petals to the sidewalk. I feel like I've stepped inside a souvenir snow globe. Walking past window after window, I'm mesmerized by each detail. Every shop is curated to a gorgeous perfection and my anxiety fades away.

I don't realize I've walked into one until a buttery voice slides next to me. "Shopping for a friend?"

This woman has the poutiest lips I've ever seen. They're so puffy I'm worried she's in the middle of an allergic reaction, but they are also perfectly coated in a glossy pink. Which means she paid for the pout. Forcing myself to stop staring at her lips, I lift my hand to a rack of shift dresses, walking my fingers across the top of the hangers to the last one. Ten, the largest size they carry. Not that I could afford anything as nice as this, but it wouldn't matter.

I swallow, unable to hide the waver in my voice. "Yep, for a friend." Of which I have zero. Suddenly I'm the most exhausted I've ever been, and I'd give anything to have a friend next to me. My lack of friends are another thing to add to my list.

Unwanted. Abandoned. Overweight. Alone.

The woman's face brightens because now I could be a customer instead of a nuisance. My phone buzzes and I pull it out, seeing the reminder I set for the meeting with my soon-to-be landlord in half an hour. Pretending it's a call, I slide my thumb over the screen and mouth, *sorry*, while louder than necessary, I answer the imaginary call. "Hey, what's up?"

Outside, I lean against the brick wall adjacent to the store I exited. Is life this hard for everyone? Does anyone else feel like they are constantly jumping over hurdles? I close my eyes and take a breath, then another, and another, keeping my eyes closed. If only I were standing at the edge of the

Pando. It's a forest of nearly fifty thousand genetically identical aspen trees, all sharing the same root system. It's one of the earth's oldest living organisms, and one day I'm going to see it for myself. When I feel like clawing my way out of my skin, I picture myself standing under these quaking limbs with their crisp golden leaves fluttering all around me. Somehow it makes me feel normal, and I have my old neighbor Sylvia to thank for that.

When I open my eyes I'm disoriented by Lambert Avenue. Soon, I'll have this street memorized, but right now it's another reminder that nothing is familiar. Beverly and her husband Calvin Lambert have been revitalizing Tinlee Bay for years. The magazine images of this town and her hotel made me envious; they are what brought me here. And now I have the perfect word to describe what I'm seeing.

Homogenous. Everything looks exactly the same. The word curdles in my stomach. It really is sour milk.

Dumping my backpack to the sidewalk, I unzip the small front pouch, extracting folded-together pages. I already have these wrinkled images committed to memory and now I smooth them flat across my leg. It was these pictures that caught my attention, which I ripped from the magazine and kept for myself instead of condemning them to the recycle bin like I was supposed to. These pictures are the reason I'm here. I read the caption for the millionth time.

Real estate investor Calvin Lambert, along with his design-savvy wife Beverly, have breathed life back into this coastal California town.

I'm here because I chose to come. But when have I ever gotten what I want?

My phone chimes with another reminder for my appointment and I push myself off the brick wall. I do not want to be late for the walk-through with my landlord. At the very least, in a few minutes, I'll have a set of keys, a place to set my backpack, and I can finally take a much needed, and extremely long hot shower.

Typing my new address into the map, I get my bearings and start walking. Beverly said she'd be in touch tomorrow. I just need to get settled, do a load of laundry, and try not to overanalyze every word she said.

Taking a left off Lambert, the sea breeze nudges my back, reminding me of afternoons when I would try to catch the wind. I ran through yards that weren't mine trying to capture something that couldn't be seen because I was young enough to believe I could. I was also young enough to believe the adults when they said, *You can be anything you want.* The thing is, beliefs like that don't belong to kids like me, and the wind is not meant to be caught. It rustled through the grass, tangled my hair, and pushed over my face, refusing to settle between the palms of my hands. Still, I chased it because I knew that once my feet crossed the threshold, the adults would say, *I'm sorry, one day this will all make sense.*

Life still doesn't make sense. When I turn to face the wind now, I'm met with a rectangular slice of dazzling blue through the tunnel of buildings and even this hindered view of the ocean takes my breath away.

"Please." I don't know who I say this to, but I whisper it again. "Please, I need this job. I need to stay here." The wind pushes my hair off my shoulders and lifts my plea up, tucking my prayer onto feathered wings, keeping it safe. Or maybe the wind is flying my request far away, farther than I'll ever be able to reach.

3

How many times have I stood outside a new house with my life stuffed into a bag, wondering what awaited me beyond the threshold? The answer is too many to count. But standing at the base of the three steps leading to the blue house with white shutters and a railing surrounding a spacious porch is different. This is not another group home, or a temporary house my social worker scrambled to find.

I did this. I found myself a place to live.

Pressing a finger to the bell, I wait until a warped outline of a person emerges through the multicolored stained glass window at the center of the door. A man opens it. His gray hair is matted on one side of his head and sprouting up on the other. The plaid shirt he's wearing isn't buttoned properly; a long triangle hangs like a tail at his thigh. He's scowling. "I don't want whatever you're selling." The door swings shut.

After today's remarks from Beverly, and the woman with puffer-fish lips, I am running out of patience, and right before the door closes, I jam my foot in its way, stopping it.

The scowl on his face deepens. "I said—"

I don't have the energy for what he's about to say. "I'm here for my appointment with Laurel. For the walkthrough."

At that, his face softens a fraction before his caterpillar eyebrows smoosh together. "Are you kidding?"

I have half a mind to push past him, find the stairs to the basement, and collapse on the bed listed in the advertisement. "Why would I be kidding?" Pulling out my phone, I tap open the emails, proof I should be here. Finding the thread, I shove my phone in his face. He starts to swat it away, but sighs, taking it, blinking at the screen, his finger slowly pushing the messages up as his shoulders fall.

When he hands my phone back, the corners of his mouth are still turned down. "Look, there's nothing I can do. But if it makes you feel any better, you're not the first one."

"First one what?"

"Being scammed," he says. "Somebody's been using my address, posting a room to rent, collecting the money online. Every few months someone new shows up thinking they are about to move in. Police have been notified, but not much they've been able to do so far. If you want, go talk to Baxter at the station. He's the one I've spoken to."

I rock back a step as if he shoved me. The police station isn't on a list of places I'd like to visit. Even if any information

I give them would help stop the scammer, I'm not going there. The police ask questions I do not like to answer.

My foot no longer wedges his front door open, and the man takes the opportunity to close it even as he's speaking. "Really am sorry but there's nothing I can do." Then the deadbolt clicks.

No matter how hard I try to rearrange the pieces of my life, they never fit. Unlike the colored pieces of cut glass on the door which all join the next one perfectly. This cannot be happening. My stomach clenches at the amount of money I lost paying the down payment for a room that was going to be my home. And what did I get instead? Absolutely nothing.

I pound my fists against the glass. "I've already paid. In advance. Three months. What am I supposed to do about that? What am I supposed to do?" I'm screaming, but I don't care.

When I finally stop smacking his door, my hands are red. He never came back, but why would he? There's nothing he can do.

I had to beg my boss for every extra house cleaning assignment I could get; some had fit into my schedule, and some didn't, which forced me to cut a few classes, just so I could Venmo the money to Laurel in time. And now I am seriously screwed.

I remember finding the listing and shoving down my initial gut reaction that it was too good to be true. *Basement room with a small kitchenette to rent, one block from the ocean. Bed, dresser, table, and two chairs provided. Laundry onsite. Street parking. No pets. No smoking.*

The rent was cheaper than anything else I'd come across and the pictures were pristine. My shoulders fall. Apparently, I'll do anything if it comes with a pretty picture. But I spoke to Laurel, or whatever her real name is, on the phone. Her voice was delicate and friendly. Not the voice of someone who was scamming me for almost every cent I had. She reassured me it was all true, and I believed her.

I know what will happen if I call her now, but I tap through my contacts until I find her name. It rings several times before a robotic-sounding voice tells me this number has been changed, disconnected, or is no longer in service. I shove the phone in my pocket instead of screaming again.

Squeezing the back of my neck with my hand, I take a deep breath but am nowhere near calm. I can't stand on this guy's porch much longer; I have to go. My backpack feels a hundred pounds heavier, just like my heart, as I head down the steps. Adjusting the straps, I walk the advertised one block to the ocean because I have no idea what else to do.

The beach is littered with pods of people. Families. Elderly couples. Girls my age wearing Daisy Dukes with frayed edges. Kids hunting for rocks or shells or other imagined treasures. Teens skim across the water's edge on what look like miniature surfboards. A shaved ice booth stands to my left with a man leaning against it, flinging pinched-off pieces of bread to a swarm of seagulls. Everything about this town is a vibe, it is so beautiful it could be a movie set.

Disappointment stabs between my ribs. I don't know how I am ever going to fit inside this scene. If I were back in Montana right now, I'd hike into the forest until the trees were so close they practically touched and stay there until my heart stopped hurting.

But I don't have a forest.

Or a home.

I only have myself, my mistakes, and my backpack.

By the time I decide to untie my shoes and venture onto the sand, the sun is a last burst of red across the water, and I've never seen anything like it.

Your neighbor is not lying when they come home from their vacation to Glacier National Park passing out stickers and hats and drink cozies all emblazoned with *Big Sky Country*. That's Montana for you. The sky is so open you feel naked in front of the gods. But this. The ocean turning itself into a wash of glittering fires is nothing short of magic, and it releases the emotions I've held back all day.

I can hardly see through my tears. They trace lines down my face, blurring the sand, the waves, and the setting sun into a pile of melted crayons. I want to lie down. I want someone to give me a hug. I want to look at the ocean and be overwhelmed with relief that I am home, instead of having my heart catch in my throat with dread, certain I'm being pulled out into a very uncertain sea.

Statistics about kids who age out of the foster system are not encouraging. Maybe the short end of the stick is all I'll ever be allowed to grasp, because here I am, staring down the barrel of being eighteen and homeless.

Squishing the sand with my toes, I wipe my face. Tears won't help, they won't change what's happened today, and I will not let myself keep crying; it's never helped me before. I could still get the job at the B Hive. It is a thin thread of hope, and I'm exhausted from trying to hold my life together, but it's all I have left to hold on to.

4

The beach is black as I walk south along the seam of sand.

I stood rooted to the ground as the night swallowed the sea. But before the last shred of the sun disappeared, I noticed dunes farther down the beach and figured they might be a good place to sleep.

Behind me, the lights of Tinlee Bay wink across the landscape, but I keep them at my back. I don't want to think about houses with families tucked inside, but I can't stop myself. There could be crackling fires and popcorn popping in the microwave. Kids will be finishing their baths and slipping into zippered pajamas, rushing with still-damp hair down the stairs to jump on the lap of an older sibling, begging for a turn on the Xbox. I stop walking, unclenching my hands that I've balled into fists. What I've imagined is a photo shoot for a commercial, not reality. I know inside those houses it's more likely to be arguments over brushing teeth and shouts of *ten more minutes of screen time or else*. I know that, but my heart still squeezes with jealousy over everything I've never had, even if none of it is real.

Closer to the dunes I catch a hint of smoke in the air. The smell of a campfire is one of my favorites, and for a moment I close my eyes to let the scent settle my rattled heart. A wave crashes and smoke lingers on the breeze, an intoxicating new combination that I want to last forever. When I open my eyes, there are faint flames flickering far in the distance and I am a moth caught by its glow.

Voices rise and fall as I approach, and every so often snatches of a song push past the edges of the conversations. There is a main bonfire with a smaller one sprouting off to the side, people passing between both. I should stop before I'm noticed, or before I'm asked who I am and why I'm here. It would be so satisfying to warm my body next to the fire, but I want more than that. I want everything the people ringing the flames have—a place to be and people to share it with.

As I inch closer, a girl asks, "Would you rather be able to move things with your mind or have the ability to read other people's thoughts?"

Answers bounce around the group and then a guy says, "Okay, okay, okay, but would you rather if people could read your thoughts, or if everyone knew your internet search history?"

The group groans and a new male voice says, "Wouldn't matter for you, Wick, they'd be the same things." The owner of this new voice shoves the guy who asked about search history in the way guys do when they're best friends and mocking each other.

There's something familiar about standing on the fringe of an established group. It happened every time I walked into a new house. I would watch the family interact, trying to figure out who would be my friend, who would find my faults, and who would get tired of me first. It was harder to tell than you might imagine. But it wasn't just that. Every house had its own smell, its own way of living life. Houses came with their own rules to Uno, and specific preference for shoes off by the door or permission to wear them in every room. I often got branded as lazy or a troublemaker for my "complete disregard for the way our family operates." But that wasn't true at all. It was just too much for me to keep track of.

"Hey." The guy I now know is Wick holds up his hands. "Don't pretend yours wouldn't be the same."

Everyone laughs and it's such a comforting sound that it pulls me closer until I'm in their midst, standing next to a girl who asks another question. "Would you rather spend a week alone in the forest or a night alone in a haunted house?"

"Forest." I didn't mean to answer, it was simply a reflex, but now everyone stares at me. My stomach clenches. So much for staying hidden in the shadows.

Wick spins to the sound of my voice. "Well hello, snack pack."

His friend shoves him, less playfully this time. "Stop calling people that."

Wick cracks his knuckles and leans around the perimeter of the fire. "Sorry. My friend Lamby says I need to stop referring to vacationers as snacks. But when you think about it, it makes perfect sense."

The girl next to me bumps her elbow into mine. "Don't listen to him." She cups her hands over her mouth, magnifying her voice. "Wick is an idiot."

Everyone hollers and Wick dips himself in a dramatic bow. "At your service. Plus, it's my birthday so I get to be an idiot if I want."

"What's your excuse for every other day?" The girl laughs. She is petite, as in, could be a gymnast. Her laugh should sound like butterfly wings, but it doesn't. It sounds like tires driving along a gravel road, the kind of road you travel all day and never see another soul.

She gathers her long hair in her hands, secures it in a messy bun on the top of her head, and stretches her fist in front of me. "I'm Lacie. And seriously, never mind birthday boy over there, he gets far too much attention for his own good." She's still basically shouting.

Wick jogs over to Lacie. "Never enough attention from you, Lacie Lau." He makes a pouty face and even in the darkness with the firelight dancing over his features I can see the playfulness in his warm hazel eyes.

"Tough break." Lacie laughs again, then plants herself

between Wick and me, staring at me like it's my turn to say something.

"Oh, hey, I'm Rindy," I say, finally bumping my fist into hers.

"So, Rindy," Wick says, "you normally go on vacation and show up to random beach parties with your luggage?" He leans his elbows onto Lacie's shoulders. "It's your parents, isn't it? You're making a break for it, am I right, or am I right?"

Tugging on the straps of my overly-stuffed, goo-filled backpack, I make it tighter on my shoulders. "My parents are ghosts—" I clamp my mouth shut. What is wrong with me? I never offer information about myself. First, it was answering the forest question, and now this. I must be more exhausted than I realized. But there is something undeniable about the ease of their banter, it's calming and it makes me want to join in. Either way, I don't want to tell strangers that I don't know who my parents are. Or that it never worked out with any of the foster families I was placed with. I know what happens when people learn that information. I become different. Plus, I moved all the way out here so that my past wouldn't interfere with my future anymore.

But I just started a very strange sentence about ghosts and my parents. Lacie's head is tipped to the side and Wick looks confused but expectant. I'm grasping for something to say, wondering how I can salvage this, and I say the first thing that comes to mind. "Writers. As in, my parents are ghostwriters." That was horrendous. I would never believe that lie. I want to cover my face.

"Okay." Wick stretches the word out then his face lights up. "Wait, are they here doing research?"

Lacie smacks the back of her hand on his chest. "What would they find to research *here*?"

"Oh you know, the usual. Infidelity a la mode." He rotates Lacie to face him. "Or they could be here scouting a location for some beach drama." He stands up taller. "Better yet, they are searching for a hotter-than-average guy to grace their next cover." His eyes dart to mine, his face beaming. "Please tell them you found their next cover model."

Lacie shoves Wick away, but not without a smile. "Go find Nolan. You're driving me crazy." She turns back to me, rolling her eyes. "He's like a puppy, needing constant attention and sometimes a stick to chew." She acts annoyed but these are her people, and maybe she doesn't know how lucky she is. "Are you visiting for the summer?" she asks.

Yes. My plan was to never leave, but at this point, I have no idea. I need to tread carefully with what I say. I don't want to tell her the truth, but I also just invented ghost-writing parents. Would it be wrong to tell her I'm here on vacation? I rub the back of one hand across my eyes and nod.

"Awesome. You seem cool," Lacie says.

I almost take a step back. I don't know why she says that because this is not a general first impression I am used to. So far all I've done is crash a birthday beach bonfire and have very awkward conversations. Maybe she's just being nice. Either way, it's not what I'm used to.

"Where are you from?" she asks.

"Montana." Some truths are too ingrained to be thrown away.

"Nice. Maybe we could hang out sometime. It would save me from spending my summer with these savages. Don't get me wrong. I love them." She looks over her shoulder, making sure Wick's attention has latched on to something else, but she lowers her voice anyway. "Don't tell Wick I said that, or he'll assume I *love* him. Which I do not." The night does not cover the glint in her eyes either.

I pull a zipper across my lips. "Secrets are my specialty."

Lacie winks, unaware of how true that is. It's quiet for a moment and she scans the bonfire as if she is looking for someone then across to the smaller fire before her eyes flare open. "Oh crap, this never ends well." She starts running. "Sorry, I'll be right back." She shouts for someone named Nolan to join her as she hurries to the other bonfire.

Wick is standing on top of an overturned log, bare-chested, and shouting, "I challenge you to a duel!"

It's strange, now that Lacie is gone, I feel cold as if she was the fire I had been standing next to. The word *friend* is a flash of lightning through my chest. What would it be like to have what Lacie has? Or to have her as my friend? I shouldn't count on it; I've never been good at making friends, or keeping them. When everyone knows every last detail about your life, it's hard to start a friendship on level ground. And if there was an opportunity, I always pushed it away because it took more energy than I was willing to expend.

But now? It's like I've never had a sip of water, and someone has offered me a glass. I want to refill the cup and drink again. I rub another hand across my face. I'm too tired to keep inventing a new life on the spot. If I stay here much longer, I'll end up mumbling other strange details about a life I've never lived. I need to find a place to sleep for the night.

The dunes are situated to the side of the bonfire so I can't exactly nestle in and close my eyes without drawing attention to myself. Climbing to the top, I hope to find a place on the other side, away from view. Below the dunes are a row of pine trees and a shadow that looks like a shed. Slipping my way down the sand, I walk toward the structure. Up close, the blue paint on the wood is peeling. It's not a very large building, there's a door that is locked and no windows, and on the side closest to the dunes is a rack housing three canoes. They are covered in cobwebs and the middle one is the worst because a patch of gray rot has made a feast of the wood, leaving a splintered hole.

Walking another circle around the small building, I check to make sure there's nothing else out here. The only other thing is a foundation of what I assume was supposed to be a house, but the edges are overtaken by grass and weeds, like it never got built. It's been abandoned for a long time and I drop my backpack to the dirt and roll my shoulders, savoring the relief of no longer having everything I own strapped to my back. Then I crawl under the lowest canoe.

It's strangely cozy, like a cocoon—I must be so far past exhaustion if the hard-packed earth under a rotting canoe is comfortable. Dragging my backpack next to me, I pull out my flannel shirt, which is more jacket than a shirt. It's all the blanket I'm going to have for the night, even if it still has globs of body butter stuck to it. Shuffling my pack up to my head, I smoosh it a few times and voila, I have a lumpy pillow.

I never expected to start my life in Tinlee Bay homeless. I was supposed to have a basement studio and a pillowtop mattress. My exhale is a loud huff. I've lived inside houses, apartments, a double-wide, and a group home, but none of those were ever mine. Most days I felt more homeless enclosed inside those rooms than I do right now. At least I'm out here doing something about my life. Even if I am failing. If I am going to crash and burn, at least I will have tried to make my life something other than the nothing I knew it would be if I stayed.

Snatches of voices from the bonfire push over the dune. I bet everyone there doesn't know how lucky they are. Or maybe they do and that's why they are out celebrating their friend. My eyes are drooping, it's been so long since I closed them and it's hard to keep them open. I miss the heat from the flames and pull the shirt tighter across me. As I do a spark lights in my chest all over again. What hole in my heart would be healed if I could call Wick and Lacie my friends?

5

For a moment I forget where I am. Then it all comes crashing back.

Scam. Homeless. Bonfire. Canoe.

Adding to this list of not-great things is the fact that it's pitch-black, and I need to use the bathroom. Which isn't that big of a deal, except I don't know where to find one. Before rolling out from under the canopy I make sure my backpack is shoved against the wall of the shed completely out of sight before setting off on my quest.

After skidding down the other side of the dune I'm face-to-face with the remnants of the party, but it's abandoned. During my time standing next to the flames, groups of girls trailed farther south and I'm hoping it means they were headed to a beach-access bathroom and not off to pee some-where in the shadows. It's as good of a guess as any and I shuffle that direction. Blissfully, in the distance, a dim light illuminates the corner of a concrete block building. I pick up my pace. When I'm close enough to see the word *women* carved into a wooden sign next to a door, I almost cry.

A harsh light flicks to life when I pull the door open, forcing me to duck my head to the side, blinking against the explosion of light. There are two stalls without doors, which is not ideal, but beggars cannot be choosers. I've never been so thankful for a bathroom in my entire life.

The sink water is ice, and after washing my hands I dry them with the tails of my flannel shirt. No mirrors grace the wall above the sink, but if I were looking myself in the eyes, I know they'd be bloodshot because they feel like sandpaper every time I blink.

Exiting the bathroom, I stand still, letting my eyes adjust to the darkness before walking back. The crisp night air wraps its wispy arms around me, filling my lungs, and every breath wakes me up a little more. Without the mission of finding a bathroom, my mind is free to wander, but that only means a new flock of worry birds begin to build a nest in my heart. What was I thinking by moving here? Why did I think I'd be able to hand-pick the life I wanted? I should've known better because what I *want*, and what I *get*, are always opposites.

A bench sits between the dunes and the restroom, so I plop down on the wooden slats. These past twenty-four hours haven't been what I expected, and it's crushing to know I'm truly on my own. There's a big difference between feeling like an unwanted third wheel within a family and knowing that if I stood up and walked into the ocean no one would know I disappeared.

Pulling one leg up to my chest, I rest my chin on my knee and close my eyes. The water rushing back and forth across the sand is such a comforting sound. And to think it's the moon, however many thousand miles away, that causes the tide to come in. Or out. I have no idea which one is happening right now, but it's amazing that something so far away can affect what is right in front of me. This better not be a metaphor for my past continuing to affect my present, no matter what I do to try to change my circumstances.

I used to play a game where I went back in time and had a do-over. The moments I chose ranged from awful interactions at school, to drama in the group home, or never agreeing to meet JP at the equipment shed before it burned to the ground. But mostly I chose to go farther back in time, to the days before I was abandoned. There is so much I would change if I could.

"Here's an interesting question, what is Forest Girl doing sitting alone on a bench in the middle of the night?" The sudden interruption of a male voice behind me sends me leaping from the bench. "Whoa, hey," he says as I spin to face him. He steps back, his hands raised in a gesture of peace. "I didn't mean to scare you."

My pulse rushes against my eardrums, drowning out the ocean at my side. This guy is tall, wearing a stripy, woven hoodie, ripped jeans, no shoes, and why does his voice sound familiar? Better yet, "What did you just call me?" I ask.

When he first spoke his voice was self-assured, but now it's hollowed out with doubt. "Aren't you ..." He steps closer. "Yeah, I thought so. From earlier." His hand flicks behind him toward where the bonfires had been. "Wick's party. You're the girl who stopped by. The one who would rather sleep alone in a forest."

My back relaxes at the mention of a multitude of trees. His voice sounded familiar because a handful of hours ago, he was the one who shoved Wick for calling me a snack pack. What did Wick call him? I pull my hair over my shoulder, twisting it together.

I remember as I take a seat on the bench again. "You're Lamby."

It sounds like a question and not a statement, but he nods, smiling while pointing to the space next to me and I dip my head in a yes.

"Nolan," he says, sitting on the bench beside me, leaving plenty of space between us.

Nolan. That's the name Lacie shouted as she ran to stop Wick from whatever challenge he wanted to face.

"Rindy," I tell him, even though he didn't ask. He drapes an arm over the empty space at the top of the bench as I pull my leg back up to my chest.

"The question still stands." Nolan pauses. "What are you doing out here all alone?"

"Couldn't sleep." It's the truth. Minus the fact it was my bladder that woke me up. Also minus the fact that I almost had to squat in the dune; those are details no one needs.

He shoves the hood off his head, ruffling a hand through hair; in the darkness I can't tell what color it is.

"What about you?" I ask. "Out prowling the beach searching for girls to scare?"

"Nope. No prowling. I was sitting." He points over his shoulder, and I follow his motion to see the shadow of a sea wall far behind us. I can picture him sitting atop it, his long legs kicking the stones as he watched me find the bench. Not that long ago, he was at his friend's birthday party. What would make him choose to stay out all alone? It's a question I don't have the right to ask. If I did, I would be hand-delivering an invitation for him to ask me about my life in return.

I push the conversation into easy waters. "Not prowling. Makes sense. Lambs aren't exactly predatory, are they?"

Nolan's laugh is a chesty rumble, and combining it with the sound of the ocean is exceptionally nice. But ever since arriving in Tinlee Bay, anything plus the ocean is the best thing I've ever experienced.

He stretches out his hand that hangs limply over the top of the bench and squeezes my shoulder. "Just when I think I've heard every lamb reference known to man, you gift me with a new one."

Smiling, I hunch forward, pressing my chin to my knee in an instinct to take up less space next to someone else. But when I do, I miss the warmth of his hand; it somehow made me feel less alone, like I was anchored to this place instead of trying to drive my own stake into the sand.

"I imagine at some point *Silence of the Lambs* references must come into play with a nickname like Lamby," I say.

"You have no idea."

A quiet settles between us, but it's not awkward. It feels as if something is connecting us. Maybe it's simply the fact we are alone together in the darkness, at the edge of the sea, that makes it easy to imagine we are the only people on the planet.

"What about you?" I ask. "Would you rather sleep alone in the forest for a week, or bunk with the Ghost Busters for a night?"

He doesn't look at me when he answers, keeping his eyes on the ocean we can hear but not see. "Easy. Forest."

There's a longing in his voice. Like he's thought about it before, not necessarily this specific question, but a longing for something else, something more. Maybe I recognize it because I've felt the same way my entire life.

Nolan is still making tunnels under the sand with his feet when he turns to me. "I know my reasons, but what makes you want to camp by yourself for a week?"

If I had been taking a sip of water, I would've sprayed it all over him. Instead, I snort loudly. One of his eyebrows ticks up in amusement at the horrible sound I made and my face flushes, but thankfully it's too dark for him to notice. He has no idea that I'll be sleeping on the ground for the foreseeable future.

My answer was an impulse, a reflex, and it was Sylvia's fault. Thinking about her brings a smile to my lips, but once again I have to be careful what I say. Somewhere between falling asleep and nature calling, I had decided that the easiest way to keep track of all the details—lies—of my new life is to stick as close to the truth as possible, without actually telling the truth.

"I had a neighbor. She's a retired Forest Ranger and lives in this tiny yellow house nestled in a grove of pines. There was always something comforting about being in the woods with her, like it's where we both belonged."

Before I got to know Sylvia, I thought it was the fact that there was more land than house on her property that I liked the best, but it wasn't that. Spending time with her made me feel more like myself than anywhere else.

Sylvia understood that there were days I would rather chew off my own arm than walk through the trees and go back to the group home. So, she'd call Gov, the man who ran it, and let me sleep on her porch. Not because I wasn't welcome inside her house, but because from the first day of April to the first frost of autumn, that's where she slept. Outside, we'd listen to the wind whispering through the trees or hear the call of a great gray owl, and I could ask her anything and she would always tell me the truth.

It's why I didn't hesitate before collapsing under a canoe rack: there's something familiar about sleeping outside.

Nolan's whole body was turned toward me as I spoke, and now he's squinting at me. Did I say something wrong? Maybe he realized he made a mistake by walking over and asking to share the bench with me. This is not a conversation normal people have. Normal people discuss the series they are binge-watching. Normal people talk about who is dating who, or their plans for the weekend, or argue over whatever new controversy happens to be trending.

Normal people don't tell strangers stories about spending time in the forest with their old neighbor.

Lies. Truth. Life. Being normal. It's all too hard for me and I press my hands to my knees and stand. "Right, well, I should probably go."

Nolan looks up at me with a frown, and it feels as if I'd been holding the string of a balloon but accidentally let go. "Wait, you can't just leave," he says. I tilt my head to the side as he keeps talking. "I mean, you're new here, I wouldn't want you to get lost." He stands up and my head has to keep tilting skyward to find his eyes. "Tell you what. If I guess the Vrbo your family is staying at, then I get to walk you home."

Walking me home cannot happen because then he would find out the truth. That I'm homeless and sleeping under a stack of canoes. But there's no rental property for him to guess. So I say, "Deal."

He chews the corner of his mouth. "Artsy parents. Staying all summer. South end of town, which is unusual." He smacks his leg. "The three-bedroom on Look Out Cove."

I have no idea what that house is like, but wish I was staying there. I wish I could tell him he guessed correctly so that this boy, who is ridiculously easy to talk to, would walk me to a house I can only dream of. He's waiting for me to answer with an open expression on his face. I'm used to people staring at me with an *I-know-all-about-you* expression. Or pity. Or worse—both.

Nolan's face carries none of that, in fact, it's the opposite.

I shrug away the idea that I'll be disappointing him, shrug away the fact that I'd like to sit down and slide back into the effortless territory of having a conversation with him. But I can't. "Sorry, that's not the one."

He gives me a half smile. "Want an escort anyway?"

This random conversation with a stranger in the middle of the night has been the best thing in my life for several days, weeks if I'm honest, but it makes my heart tighten. Back home there were never any strangers in my life, everyone knew all there was to know about me, just like I knew all there was about them; the curse of small towns. And everyone I knew decided that one single detail would define my life. I was found inside a box and spent the rest of my life living inside the box they built for me. A box labeled, *not worth it.*

When I set out to leave my past in the past, I never considered what it would feel like to have someone want to get to know me. And now I have no idea how to fit that into the life unfolding before me, especially with all these unexpected holes that I don't know how to fill in and smooth over.

I need a job.

I need a place to live.

I need a friend. My heart thumps. Friends are a luxury, not a need. "That's okay, I can make it on my own," I say.

It's one hundred percent the truth, and not just for

tonight. I have no other option but to make it on my own, I have no backup plan, and there is no safety net. My feet falter in the loose sand as I walk away. I half expect Nolan to fall into step beside me, and I convince myself I'm not disappointed when he doesn't. The truth is, he can't come with me, or we'd be forced to walk in circles the rest of the night, because there's no way I'm revealing to Nolan where I'm sleeping.

Right before I'm lost in the shadows, Nolan calls out, "See you around."

And I can't help but wonder what might happen if he does.

6

When I first stepped off the Greyhound in Tinlee Bay, I was met with sea air and a rush of possibility. But so far, it's been one disaster after another. And now no matter how hard I try, I cannot fall back asleep. My mind is alive and racing from my encounter with Nolan, not to mention the same doubts that bubbled to the surface when I first sat on the bench. A long list of failures is tying me into a knot.

Once a week at Gov's house we had a movie night. It was never mandatory, but every girl showed up because having two hours to numb out in front of a screen was better than nothing. When we watched *Cast Away*, I practically took notes—this is how you survive—always travel with an inflatable raft on your lap.

Underneath the canoe, I clutch my backpack to my chest, realizing I've packed the wrong things. There is no inflatable raft in sight, and my plane is going down. How is this happening? These plans should have been my very own raft, pulling me to the surface where I could finally catch a break.

So far, my plans have amounted to nothing.

I check the time on my phone. It's four in the morning and another worry slams into my chest. How am I going to charge my phone? Not only that, how am I going to keep paying for it? My stomach twists and I power it off. Beverly is not going to call and offer me a job in the middle of the night, so I might as well conserve the battery while I can. When the sun rises, I'll turn it back on for the day. But after I find out one way or another about the job at the B Hive, I'll have to cancel my cell service so I can save as much money as possible.

Friends are a luxury and so are phones.

When the sky is a light gray, I pull my backpack out from under the canoe. There's no point lying under it anymore. I want a long, hot shower more than anything, but I only have one option.

Thankfully the beach access bathroom door has a deadbolt and I twist it, hoping no early morning beachcomber will be in need. Shrugging my backpack to the floor, I strip as quickly as possible. To say I feel exposed standing naked in this shockingly bright cinderblock room is the understatement of the year.

Finding a random T-shirt from inside my pack, I shove it under the flow of what must be glacier water and start scrubbing my body. Soap would be nice, but I didn't pack any and the container mounted to the wall is empty. I'm shivering, my skin is blotchy red from the cold and the scrubbing, and I haven't even done the worst part.

I huff out three quick breaths before forcing my head under the water. Clenching my eyes shut, I scrape my nails along my scalp as fast as I can, but my fingers are already numb and my head feels like a pincushion, every drip of water stabs. I can't stand it any longer, and maybe it's a good thing I don't have any soap because I'm not sure I could keep my head under long enough to rinse it.

Dripping water on the floor, I use my flannel shirt as a towel before wrapping it turban style on my head. Extracting the least lotion-covered shirt and leggings I can find, I discover a pair of underwear with no lotion splotches at all. It's the first bit of luck I've had in days. Never underestimate the power of a clean pair of underwear. I am a woman reborn.

But I'm still in need of several things, and a laundromat is my next priority.

Not many street signs point the way in this section of Tinlee Bay. I guess you need to know where you are. What did Nolan say last night? That it was strange my pretend family and I are staying in the southern part of town. Is this where the locals live? The buildings here are far less impressive than the ones populating Lambert Avenue; I would even say they are slightly run-down. Not a single well-lit, one-of-a-kind specialty shop to be seen here.

I turn my phone on long enough to search for a laundromat and then power it back off once I'm headed in the right direction.

Oh Suds Up is squashed between a used bookstore and a locksmith. The letters are a peeling maroon in need of a fresh coat of paint. Testing the door, I find it swings open freely and I whisper a thank you to the twenty-four-hour laundromat gods. There's not much inside. A cracked orange vinyl bench sits in front of the window, a table for folding clothes is in the middle of the room, and an empty magazine rack and a trash can are the only things in the room beside a bank of washing machines and dryers. But next to the dust-collecting wire rack is an electrical outlet. Unwinding my charging cord, I plug in my phone, thankful it can charge while I wash.

After all my clothes and my backpack have been washed, I fold everything I own back into place and turn on my phone.

No missed calls.

No messages.

It is only seven in the morning. Today is going to be a very long day.

Back in the heart of Tinlee Bay, I camp on a bench that overlooks the ocean and watch seagulls swoop and tilt. I don't believe in luck; why should I, when everything has failed me? But I'm not above crossing my fingers to will my phone to ring. It doesn't work.

I've sat here long enough to watch a runner on the beach disappear and then finally return. Long enough for the sun to be high in the sky, warming my back. Long enough to wonder if I should get up and stretch my legs or sit on this bench all day when my phone finally rings.

An unknown number flashes on my screen with the correct area code for Tinlee Bay. *This is it. Please let this be good news.*

"Hello, Rindy, this is Beverly." I hold my breath as she continues. "I'm so glad I caught you. I've decided to offer you the job." It is exactly what I wanted, but my lungs won't work. I'm frozen, holding my breath, listening to the silence stretch between us. "That is if you're still interested."

I jump from the bench, my heart racing, the air rushing out of me as if I've been slammed to the ground. "Yes. Thank you. Thank you. Thank you." I say it to the universe, to the crashing waves, to the arching seagulls, and again to Beverly. "Thank you, I accept. Wow, yes, this is perfect." I sound like a babbling idiot, but I don't care. I've gone from having everything stripped out of my hands to holding on to a single strand of hope and I'm not letting go of it. Maybe I have a life raft after all.

"Excellent. You can start tomorrow. Be at my office at seven a.m. If you could stop by today and sign some paperwork that would help."

The B Hive sprouts from the side of the hill, hovering over the town. It's far enough away to look like a mirage but I know it's real. I've stared at the pictures enough times to have the whitewashed walls with ebony trim encasing every window and door seared into my mind. Now I'm finally going to be a part of it. Everything is going to be okay. I will make this work, homeless or not.

"I'll head there right now. Thank you again," I say. Does Beverly sense the relief in my voice?

"Well then, welcome to the Hive."

The call ends and a laugh surges out. This must be what whiplash feels like. I have a job. And having a job means a paycheck, and a paycheck means I can find another place to live. I'll just need to be very careful.

7

This time when I walk into the main lobby of the B Hive, I'm wearing the outfit I wish I was able to slip into for my interview—a cream blouse tucked into my curve-hugging black pencil skirt. It's a major improvement from an overworn Smokey the Bear, who I smothered to death in the depths of my backpack.

A table sits next to the giant stone fireplace, and on it are complimentary honey and lavender scones, along with a coffee carafe. My stomach rumbles, reminding me I haven't eaten anything since I downed an energy drink on the bus. I'm about to grab one of the scones when a woman appears at the edge of the reception desk and calls my name. I'll have to grab one on the way out; they are free, after all.

The woman doesn't bother with chitchat, she simply hands me a clipboard of paperwork and I sit. It should be relatively easy. These are questions everyone knows the answer to. Name. Address. Birthday.

I swallow the lump in my throat and use Sylvia's address since I don't have one. Then I break into the same cold sweat I always do when writing my birthday. I don't know the day I was born. Nobody does. The thirty-first of May is not the day I was born—it's the day I was found. According to the news report I uncovered on the internet when I was twelve, I didn't have an umbilical cord, which, thanks to another search meant I was two or three weeks old when the night manager found me.

Starting on the first day of May I used to light a match every day, wondering if something would spark inside my chest, a primal knowledge of the day I first breathed air. But all that ever happened was me singeing the tips of my fingers.

The woman in Human Resources doesn't bat an eye at my birthday or the fact that I left the emergency contact line empty, all she cares about is that I have a valid social security number that I've had memorized for years. She smiles, then hands me a slip of paper detailing the approved items I'm allowed to wear to work. I suck in a breath.

A gold smock apron will be provided, but I need black shoes and shirts. Thankfully I have black leggings in spades, so I don't have to spend my money on those. But now I need to go shopping. I can't afford anything from one of the downtown boutiques, and even if I could it wouldn't fit. I have no idea if there's a secondhand store anywhere, but I know for a fact that anything I find there would not be up to Beverly's standard. I don't think Beverly approves of Walmart, but it's either that or nothing.

Folding myself onto the bench outside the main entrance of the hotel, I shove the list under my thigh and log into my bank account. I feel like I might pass out. $67.02 is all I have until I get paid at the end of the month. And that is two weeks away. Spending money on these approved items will put me further behind. But what can I do? If I don't buy them then I will not have a uniform, and if I do not have a uniform I do not have a job.

"Another day, another bench," says a voice in front of me.

Nolan leans against the valet parking podium, wearing the same woven hoodie and ripped jeans as last night. A half smile arches his lips.

My heart is an avalanche of fear. I have less than seventy dollars to my name, a crumpled shopping list under my leg, and Nolan is staring at me. To him, I'm a carefree vacationer, and despite my bank balance, I don't have to twist a smile on my face—seeing him brings one naturally. But I do have to ignore the gnawing pit in my stomach as I push my hair behind my ear.

"Well, the bench options around town seem to be frequent. I was thinking about ranking them," I say, patting the wood slats before standing, crumpling the paper that was shoved under my leg, and stuffing it into a side pouch of my backpack. "It's a solid eight."

Nolan's lips turn down in a disapproving frown, but his

eyes glint. "An eight? I don't think management would approve."

Last night I couldn't tell what color Nolan's eyes are, but they are a startling blue. Gov used to make a fire pit to burn the piles of junk mail the group home accumulated. Sometimes he'd cut a piece off an old garden hose and put it inside a copper pipe, dropping it right in the center of the flames. Pretty soon an array of colors would appear, turning the fire into an aurora borealis. Green tips curled up and out, begging you to watch, but nestled deep in the flames was an irresistible blue—the same shade as Nolan's eyes.

Tearing my focus away from the color-infused flames was always difficult, and it feels the same now with Nolan. "Well, we just won't tell management, will we," I say.

Nolan doesn't break the stare that binds us, the crescent moon of a smile still playing on his lips. I smooth my hands down the front of my skirt for something to do as a car is driven up the horseshoe driveway and the valet exits, but Nolan ignores the man wearing a pinstripe vest at his side.

I clear my throat. "Okay, well, I should go, so. See ya around." It takes me a moment to turn on my heels and start walking away, but I do. My day does not have room for Nolan or reminders of smoldering blue fires. I need to get a bus to Eureka and spend money I do not want to spend.

"Off on a big adventure?" Nolan asks.

"If you consider hopping on a bus to take me to Walmart in Eureka a big adventure, then yes." As soon as I say it, I bite the inside of my cheek so hard I'm sure I've bitten a hole in the flesh. Is this something a vacationer would say? Would they need to catch a bus to Walmart? I'm normally very good at keeping details to myself, but it's so easy to fall into a conversation with Nolan.

He's at my side now. "This is perfect. I was headed into Eureka. I'll give you a lift."

I squint my eyes at Nolan and then focus on the car behind him. It's not just any car. "You drive a Tesla?"

He scratches a hand through his dark hair. "Nope. My mechanic is holding my truck hostage at his shop, so I'm forced to borrow my mom's car." He kicks a tire.

I squint my eyes. Forced to borrow a Tesla. Who is he? Riding with Nolan would save time, but most importantly it would save the cost of a bus ticket. It would be nice if a round-trip ticket to Eureka didn't threaten to push me into the red, but I'm teetering on the edge and every cent saved is worth it.

"A ride would be nice, thanks," I say.

"Do you need to check with your parents?" That stops me from moving forward. Nolan's smile is so big it might crack his face in half. He points to the main door of the B Hive. "Not a Vrbo. Also a decent hike from the beach last night." Nolan cocks his head.

Of course, he thinks I'm staying here, why else would I be sitting in front of the main entrance? Would a simple no be all right, or do I have to dream up a bigger explanation as to why I don't need to consult my parents before hopping into his car? I shake my head, stepping closer to the Tesla.

If Nolan is bothered by my lack of explanation, he doesn't show it. "Want me to put that in the trunk?" he asks.

My backpack is an appendage I no longer notice. I have become Atlas. Not like I led a rebellion against Zeus, but here I am still being punished for existing, forced to carry my entire universe on my back. Any chance I get to slip it from my shoulders is a welcome relief.

The drive south is breathtaking. There are stretches where the ocean expands out my window and there are times when all I get are snatches of it flashing through the trees. My favorite snapshot is a craggy peak that juts from the water with pine trees sprouting like hair atop its head. "It looks like a motivational poster," I say.

"What?" Nolan asks.

"The view. It's like those motivational posters in doctor's offices."

He nods. "Be all you can be."

The flashes of the ocean through the trees continue to take my breath away. Or maybe it's the shopping spree I'm about to go on that is making it hard to take a full breath. "No, that's the slogan for the Army."

"Right." Nolan is quiet for a moment before offering, "Visualize success."

"Exactly."

Wouldn't it be nice if life were that easy? If I could close my eyes and imagine the life I wanted, and it would materialize in front of me. I exhale a huff of air. I didn't just visualize a new life, I cut out pictures of exactly what I wanted.

So much for that working. I lean my head against the window and stick to enjoying the view instead of visualizing any other details about my life, because I would probably mess those up too.

When Nolan pulls the car in front of Walmart he says, "Is it okay if I come back in about an hour? I have to go convince my mechanic to actually fix my 4Runner."

I instantly relax. I wasn't sure what I would have done if Nolan parked and decided that strolling through the aisles with me was how he wanted to pass his time. "Perfect." With my backpack securely strapped on once again, I lean down to the passenger window he rolled down and say, "Thanks again."

What I love about Walmart is that they all look the same. I could be in Eureka or Missoula or who knows where and I'd be able to find my way. But it does come with a strange sense of déjà vu. I expect to see familiar faces, or at the very least, have the store populated by Wranglers, but there are a lot more sandals and skin than boots and jeans here.

I need a pair of black shoes and one pair of size eight black canvas shoes dangle from the rack by the elastic string binding the left and right together. A yellow clearance sticker on the tag stares me in the face. $6.99 is exactly what I want to spend on a pair of shoes, but I also know how physically taxing housekeeping is and my feet would be dead after half a day's work wearing these.

Spending twenty dollars on a pair of sneakers isn't what you would call indulgent, but I'm having a hard time pushing down the panic that keeps rising in my chest as I fling the pair I just tried on into the cart.

Next on my list is shirts. The one black T-shirt I own has Bob Marley's face in a rush of rainbow colors front and center. If unhomogenous was a word that shirt would be the definition. I pull a stack of five plain black T-shirts off the shelf and weigh them, and my options, in my mind. Sweat seeps through my cream blouse. Each shirt is slightly over seven dollars and when I do the math my stomach rolls. Having five would be ideal, it would allow me to make it through a week of work and hit Oh Suds Up for a refresh on my day off, but I can't spend thirty-five dollars on shirts, so I only keep two.

I torture myself as I steer my cart through Home Goods, running my hands over the bundles of sheets I have no bed for. The endcap is a rainbow array of washcloths on sale at seventy-seven cents each. At that price, they will feel like sandpaper, but I grab a sky-blue one. Down the next aisle, I find a sandpapery bath towel for five dollars and stare at it for longer than you can imagine. Using my flannel shirt as a towel is something I don't want to repeat, and drip-drying in a locked public bathroom is not going to happen. But my purchases are adding up. Do I really need a towel? I close my eyes and toss it in the cart.

A few rows over I pick up a generic bar of soap, then round another corner for a plastic container to keep it in. Out of the corner of my eye, I catch a standing toothbrush holder, and my grasp slips off the push bar of the shopping cart as I bend forward trying to catch my breath.

Toothbrush holders mean you have a place, they mean you are welcome and wanted and that you are staying where you are. I've never had space in my life for a toothbrush holder, always keeping my toothbrush in my backpack because once I kept it on the bathroom counter and accidentally left it behind when the placement ended. It took two weeks of fuzzy teeth to build up the courage to ask for a new toothbrush. Those parents felt horrible I waited so long to ask, but sometimes the simplest requests made people upset; how was I supposed to know?

Shoving the cart toward the checkout, my stomach growls and I remember the free scones in the lobby. If only I remembered to grab one on my way out. I need food, and not just today, but for the rest of the week. Fresh food is out of the question since I don't have a place to store it, so I don't bother walking past the stacked bananas, avocados, apples, and pears. Instead, I opt for boxes of protein bars. Strawberry cream for breakfast and peanut butter delight for dinner. Each box has six bars. The more expensive boxes only have four, go figure.

Pressing both my palms to my temples, I let out a breath. I do not need to get wound up over this. But seriously would it kill their profit margins to make a box with seven bars? One box. One week. I squeeze my palms harder against the sides of my head, filling my lungs with a new breath, trying to imagine myself standing under the quaking leaves of the

Pando. It works for a moment, but the leaves transform into dollar bills and a rushing wind blows them all away.

The right front wheel of my shopping cart doesn't touch the floor, and it spins circles as I make my way to the checkout counter. Spinning. Spinning. Spinning. Exactly like my head, my heart, and my bank account. Does anyone else pushing their cart past me feel like they are on a treadmill going backward? Am I going to have enough in my account to cover everything in my cart? What should I put back if I don't? What happens when I survive by only eating protein bars? That question makes me steer my cart back toward the rows and rows of food and I snatch pouches of applesauce off the shelf as an insurance policy against scurvy. But I'm not convinced I have enough money and put them back.

One week without fruit isn't going to make my gums bleed—is it?

Why is life so hard?

My heart is racing when the cashier hands me my receipt, and I try to center myself with a thought loop as I shove my purchases into my backpack. *I start work tomorrow. I get paid in fifteen days. I start work tomorrow. I get paid in fifteen days.* But fifteen days with $3.75 left in my account makes me want to vomit. I shouldn't have any other expenses. I can last. I'll be careful. I'll cut every protein bar in half so they last longer. I can do this. I have to.

But outside I slump to the bench in front of the store and lean forward until my head is between my knees, which is not an easy task while wearing a pencil skirt, but it's the only thing that starts to regulate my breathing. Until a horn honks in front of me and I whip my head up.

Nolan's eyes are shining, but the state of me hunched into a ball outside of Walmart must concern him because he's out of the car leaning over me. "Are you okay? What happened?" he asks.

What happened? What happened is that I spent everything except $3.75 in my bank account. Tears are accumulating and I wish I had sunglasses to pull over my eyes. I sit up, straightening my spine. I will not cry. "Nothing. I'm fine. It's just the post-Walmart exhaustion," I say.

Nolan whistles. "That bad, huh?" He narrows his eyes.

Maybe he doesn't believe me, but he doesn't press the matter, and I force a smile again. Thankfully my legs don't give out when I stand. "I'll survive," I say.

It just doesn't feel like I will.

On the drive back to Tinlee Bay, I don't pay attention to the view, or the song that flits through the speakers. The only thing inside my head is a question I don't know how to answer. How am I going to survive the rest of the month on less than four dollars? Have I dug myself a hole I'll never be able to climb out of?

Suddenly Nolan nudges my shoulder. "So do you?"

I wasn't listening. Has he been talking to me this whole time? I shake my head. "Sorry, do I what?"

"Wick just texted, and he's headed to Alli Cats. He

wants me to stop by. Do you want to come too?" When I don't answer, Nolan licks his lips. "Trust me, you need to."

I try to stare at Nolan without making it clear that I'm staring at him. The list of things I need is a tourniquet around my heart. Whatever Alli Cats is, I don't actually need, but to be polite I ask, "What is it?"

Even in the reflection of the windshield where I'm pretending to not look at him, Nolan's smile is dangerous. "I could tell you. Or. I could show you."

8

Back in Tinlee Bay, Nolan drives down a street I recognize because we pass Oh Suds Up before he turns down a side street and parks. I expect to cross the street and keep walking, but he points to the right and we turn, walk half a block, and turn again. Lights are strung across the top of the alley, and it is packed with food trucks, people, and several picnic tables. Nolan turns his back on the scene and spreads his arms wide. "Welcome to Alli Cats."

From out of nowhere Wick pounces on Nolan's back. "Took you long enough," Wick says.

Nolan shrugs and twists until Wick is off his back, then holds Wick in a headlock for a few seconds before shoving him away with a smile. "We were in Eureka," Nolan says.

Wick snaps his head up. "We? We who?" Then Wick sees me and his face brightens. "Ah, Rindy, the crasher of birthdays. Welcome." It seems like Wick might bow, but he doesn't.

"You remembered my name," I say, shocked.

Wick taps his temple. "I keep every name of every beautiful girl I've ever met locked up here." Nolan shoves Wick and Wick slaps Nolan's back. "Lacie snagged us a table." Wick motions us to follow.

They walk toward a grouping of tables, but I don't move. This is exactly what I wanted when I invaded their bonfire— a place to be and people to share it with—and here I am being invited, but this feels more intrusive than crashing their party. They don't know who I am, and if they did, they wouldn't want me hanging out with them. It's a story I've lived my entire life.

A lion must be trapped inside my stomach because the rumble it makes is a roar. I've been so consumed with stress that I've forgotten how hungry I am. But now, standing here, bombarded by the smell of fried bread and tacos and brisket and I don't know what else, my body is reminding me just how hungry I am. But I cannot pay for lunch.

"I should go," I say. I can't stand the idea of staying with them and watching them eat while my stomach keeps protesting.

Nolan looks over his shoulder at me. "Aren't you hungry?" he asks. Tears threaten to return so I bite my lip to keep them from spilling, but I nod. "Well, see, there you go, the perfect reason to stay."

Wick pulls Nolan into a headlock of his own. "Plus,

Nolan never invites anyone, and we have this strange custom, more of a tradition actually. But if there's an Alli Cat newcomer joining us for lunch, then Nolan has to pay. For everyone. Isn't that right?" Wick releases Nolan, pressing his hand to his heart. "Nolan is very honor-bound and would be shattered if this opportunity slipped through his fingers," Wick says, running backward a few steps with his hands up as if he's waiting to catch a football, but it's Nolan's wallet he catches.

Nolan smiles at me. "I'm going to regret tossing that to him, aren't I?"

A laugh squawks out of me as I follow Nolan to the table. Who are these guys? How are they so full of welcome, acceptance, and kindness? Nolan can borrow a Tesla, and throw his wallet at his best friend without hesitation. I want to be annoyed by these facts, they make him sound entitled, but everything I've seen of Nolan so far as a person doesn't make me believe it's true. Even so, I don't want to be in Nolan's debt. I already owe him for a car ride and now lunch. I'll find a way to pay him back, but I'd be lying if I said today's turn of events isn't exactly what I needed.

Lacie is hunched over a sketch pad at a picnic table. When Nolan slides onto the bench next to her, she just loops her arm through his and keeps drawing whatever she is drawing. Nolan gently takes the pencil out of her grasp, her eyes meeting his in annoyance before he points her pencil toward me. Lacie's eyes go from scrunched to saucers as she jumps from her seat and wraps me in a hug. "It's you! Rindy, right?"

She spins back to her seat, and the tips of her jet-black hair flash electric blue. "You picked a good time to exit stage left last night," she says. "Duels plus Wick always equals chaos. How did he even have a jar of strawberry jam? Do you know what strawberry jam and sand turn into? Disgusting." She closes her eyes while brushing her hands in the air as if to rid herself of the memory. "Anyway. Good call for leaving." She rests her head on Nolan's shoulder, pushing the pad of paper toward me as I sit down, and I wonder if they are dating. "Something's not right with this. What's missing?" she asks.

Lacie feels like a radio turned all the way up playing my favorite song and I can't help but like her. I can't help but like being drawn into the current that swirls Lacie, Nolan, and Wick together. Life should always feel like this.

Lacie sketched an empire waist dress. I don't know what it's missing, but in general, I know what dresses lack. "Pockets," I say.

Lacie grabs her pencil from Nolan, adding dashes and notes to the sketch. "Genius."

Wick walks toward us making some sort of trumpet fanfare with his lips. The amount of food he sets on our table is ridiculous and smells delicious.

Lacie is about to grab something, but Wick smacks her hand away. "Guests first," he says.

All three watch as I select. There are tacos, ribs soaked in sauce, pulled pork with stacks of cornbread, spring rolls, and diamond-shaped fried dough topped with coconut shavings.

I choose a taco with grill marks on the tortilla. A pile of

cilantro covers the chopped meat, and it drips with sauce. I don't mean to, but when I take a bite, I close my eyes and moan.

"Amen," Wick says as everyone grabs something to eat.

We've been stuffing our faces for a while when Wick speaks again. "If you could be anywhere in the world right now, where would it be?" I like Wick's curiosity, and his constant undefined questions that feel random, but also meaningful.

Without pausing to consider, Lacie says, "Milan."

Swallowing my bite, I answer, "The Pando."

Nolan throws a wadded-up napkin that bounces off Wick's chest. "Did you put her up to this?" Nolan asks, his attention turning to me. "Did he put you up to that?"

Wick smacks the table, talking around a half-chewed bite. "Voodoo magic, that's what that was. Who even knows what the Pando is? A panda? Yes. Bamboo. Cute. China. But the Pando?" Wick shakes his head, laughing as he leans closer to me, his head almost on my shoulder. "Lamby's been talking about going to the Pando for years." Wick draws out the last word. "He has a master plan and you better believe the Pando is step one."

Nolan's fire eyes are locked on mine. "How did ... why?"

I know why he's stumbling over his question. Wick is right, no one ever knows anything about the Pando. The same strange voodoo magic rushes through my blood too. I've never met anyone who wants to go there.

He is asking me how I even know about the Pando. "Sylvia," I answer.

Nolan grabs another napkin, replacing the one he threw. "Forest Ranger neighbor. Makes sense."

Lacie and Wick exchange a glance. "Are we missing something? How does any of this make sense?" Lacie asks Nolan.

Before shoving his last bite into his mouth Nolan simply says, "Last night."

Wick jumps from the bench. "Now I know why you both disappeared from my party." He leans back, mimicking shooting a basketball. "Lamby shoots, he scores!"

"Shut up," Nolan says, throwing another napkin.

I still wonder why Nolan left Wick's party. That's not something a best friend would do, and these two are definitely best friends. Well, three, really. Ever since meeting them, it's been the three of them tied together in a knot of memories and laughter. I don't remember Nolan at the bonfire other than when I first arrived. What would make him disappear? Did he leave to sit on that seawall? Why would he want that over spending time with his friends?

But I don't ask those questions. I ask something else. "You're going to the Pando? I've always wanted to see it." I wonder if Nolan's face reflects mine. Confusion mixed with excitement from finding someone who understands the mysterious allure of a grove of swaying aspens.

Lacie answers with a sound somewhere between a sigh

and a grunt. "He's leaving us. Running away. He'll forget all about us and never come back."

Nolan grabs Lacie's hand. "That's not going to happen, I've already told you that." His eyes find mine. "I've always wanted to see it too. The pictures I've seen are incredible and I'm sure they don't do it justice." He picks up another napkin, fiddling with it between his hands. When he speaks again, his voice sounds less sure. "I'm not running away. I'm—"

"Lamby's striking out on his own, hobo style." Wick drums his fingers on the table. "Vagabond. Now there's a solid word. Lamby's gonna be a vagabond." Wick shoves a bite of whatever he is eating in his mouth.

"I'm not a vagabond. I have a job. Two, actually," Nolan says.

Lacie swipes crumbs off the sketchbook she never moved when the food arrived. "You're leaving and that's all that matters," she says.

"When are you leaving?" I don't like how spiderweb-thin my question sounds. I met Nolan yesterday, he could leave tomorrow and it shouldn't make any difference to me.

Nolan wads another napkin. "At the end of the summer."

Wick offers more, around a half-chewed bite of fried bread. "Lamby's off to prove himself."

I scrunch my eyebrows. "Why do you always call him Lamby?"

"Because Nolan Christoper Lambert is a mouthful," Wick says.

Nolan Christopher Lambert. Nolan Christopher Lambert. His name spirals through my brain. Nolan Christopher Lambert. Nolan Christopher Lambert.

Nolan, who happened to be at the B Hive this morning borrowing a Tesla. I was too caught up in my shopping-spree anxiety to wonder why. But now a firework of clarity explodes inside my brain, fizzling through my chest.

Nolan Christopher Lambert told me the car belonged to his mom, and that can only mean one thing.

Beverly Lambert—owner and chief aesthetic operator—of the B Hive is Nolan's mom.

Beverly Lambert, who starting tomorrow, will be my boss.

Beverly Lambert is the only person in Tinlee Bay who knows the truth that I am not here on vacation. And from my experience, when someone knows the truth, they use it to burn your life to ashes.

9

I can't fall asleep. Every time I close my eyes I see Nolan. He stands in front of me, a taco in one hand, the other balled into a fist, and his face twists and curves, morphing into Beverly's face. Only the eyes stay the same. Beverly's face. Nolan's voice. Asking me, *Who are you?*

An exhausted liar with bloodshot eyes, that's who I am.

Under my canoe, I wonder what would happen if I simply told everyone the truth. What would I lose? What would I gain? Maybe everything and possibly nothing. So, I lie there unable to sleep, watching an invisible source soak up the black of the sky, leaving it gray to match my mood.

A cold sink shower does nothing to improve my state of mind. And when I walk up the hill for my first day of work I'm still shivering, wishing I had a cup of coffee to wrap my hands around. But coffee costs money and being cold is free.

It turns out that Beverly likes to personally welcome all

her new employees with a chat in her office. I shouldn't be surprised since she also likes to personally interview everyone who works for her. This time, as I sit in the chair opposite her—wearing my approved clothes, new gold apron draped across my lap—I'm not distracted by the fact that I'm face-to-face with *the* Beverly Lambert. I'm distracted by my vision of Nolan's face changing into hers, and the fact that she knows the truth. Well, some of it.

My mind wanders as she gives a brief history of the B Hive, saying something about core values, and that her door is always open.

She ends by asking, "Do you have any questions?"

My mind happens to be a tornado of questions.

How close is your relationship with your son? Did you ask him what he did yesterday afternoon, or who he spent it with? Better yet, do you know he gave me a ride in your car? What would you think about that? Did you know your son bought me lunch? Or that he thinks I'm staying here on vacation with a family I don't have?

I can't ask these questions, but they have been a storm in my head since yesterday afternoon. I shake my head in response to Beverly. I have no questions I could possibly ask her, and she smiles, standing from behind her desk. "Excellent. Shall we?"

My backpack leans against the leg of my chair and I grab it as I stand. Thankfully Beverly never asked about it, but I had a ready-made lie about needing a change of clothes for after work. Which is true, but also not the whole truth. I couldn't bring myself to leave it under the canoe unsupervised all day. I follow her out of her office and we cross the lobby, past the bank of elevators to a door marked Housekeeping.

A linen cart props the door open, and Beverly taps one red lacquered fingernail against the doorframe. "Mina, this is Rindy." A person leans over the edge of a matching linen cart inside the room, her head popping up at the sound of her name. Mina has a wide smile revealing a gap between her two front teeth and brown curls escaping the bun atop her head. Beverly turns to me. "Mina will take it from here." And with that, Beverly leaves, her welcoming duty complete.

Mina waves me into the room. She talks fast, each sentence rolling into the other without a formal separation. "This is your locker," she says, tapping a metal door, and I can't believe my good luck. I can keep my belongings locked here and only carry what I need from day to day. "The combination is on the paper taped to the door. Beverly can open and search any time she sees fit. A few years ago, one of the girls kept lost and found items stashed in hers. Tried to sell them on eBay."

Mina walks a circuit of the room while she speaks. "Here's where we park our carts. Supplies. Sheets. Towels. Time clock. Trash." I'm thankful for Mina's run-on sentence way of talking; it leaves little space for any of my questions to bloom inside my brain. "I'll let you put your things away, then introduce you to Hector," she says.

Turns out Hector is my cart. Mina calls her cart Norma.

They were her grandparents' names, and I decided right then that I like Mina. Any adult who is willing to admit they name inanimate objects after family members seems like a ten out of ten. She shows me how to stock Hector with the same rolling wave of instructions.

"Heavy items on the bottom. That's your bed sheets. Next shelf, large bath towels, and robes. Top shelf is for your face towels, hand towels, bathmats, pillow cases. Tray at the top, room restocking supplies." She pats each item that is stacked to precision. "Tissues. Shampoo. Water bottles. Coffee and tea packets. Room slippers." Running her hand down the side, she says, "Cleaning supplies and garbage." Waving her hand to the other side. "Dirty linen."

She looks at me with a *simple-as-that* nod, handing me a sheet of paper with my assigned rooms to clean for today.

"We'll do your first one together, then off you go," she says.

Cleaning hotel rooms is different than cleaning houses, but it's also exactly the same. Somehow the repetitive motion of every task eases my mood just like listening to Mina talk. There is little room left in my brain as I try to get each room perfect. And fourteen rooms later, my first shift at the B Hive is done. My body is tired but in a good way, better than just being sore from waking up on the ground. At least today I earned the tightness in my shoulders, and I'm proud of my hard work. My mind spins with hope now. *I get paid in fourteen days. I can make it. I get paid in fourteen days. I can make it.*

By the time I park Hector in the stock room, I've completely forgotten about Nolan's eyes and all the questions I can't answer. Mina leans against the wall as I hang my apron in my locker. "You did good today. Picked it up faster than I expected."

Clicking the door closed, I say, "Thanks."

She smiles. "Any chance you're headed into town?" I nod as she pushes off the wall. "Want to do me a favor and drop this off at St. Andrew's?" She nudges a box with her foot.

"What is it?" I ask.

"Unclaimed lost and found. When the box is full, we take it to the church."

One of the best things about working with Mina is that she never once asked me anything personal about myself. To be fair we hadn't spent much time together after we cleaned the first room, and that was filled with her giving me instructions. We passed in the hall, but that was it. Still, I have a feeling that even if she had asked a bunch of questions, and I told her the truth, the whole truth, she would have shrugged and kept on cleaning.

Mina gives the box another nudge, sliding it into my foot, allowing me to see past the flap to a wool blanket folded at the top. I imagine a family carting this blanket to the beach to watch the sunset, or sit in front of a bonfire, and I know exactly who could use a nice warm blanket like that.

Picking up the box, I double-check, "St. Andrew's?" When Mina nods, I add, "Just as long as these things don't show up on eBay, right?"

Mina shakes her head, sending a few loose curls swinging. "See. What did I say? You pick things up faster than most." Her next words hit my back because I'm already walking away. "Bright and early tomorrow and we'll do it all again."

I don't need to ask for directions to St. Andrew's. It was the first thing I saw when I arrived in town. The church is a large brick building across the street from the bus station. Before climbing the steps to the church, I stop, unzip my backpack, and shove the blanket inside. There's enough room for it now since my clothes are living inside my locker. I'm half tempted to keep the tie-dye hoodie that's hiding under the blanket, Tinlee Bay stamped across the chest. An extra layer of warmth at night would be nice, but I don't want to risk taking too much. The blanket is all I really need.

After the rest of the items are deposited, I walk south, navigating my way through streets without signs. I want to get familiar with the side streets, try to learn more routes back to my canoes. Routes that don't involve walking on the overpopulated beach where I might find a certain boy who likes to loiter on the southern seawall. On the last residential street, I notice recycle bins set against the curb waiting to be collected. One has a very large cardboard box leaning against it. I'm five, then ten, steps away when I stop and go back. Surely if I take someone's recycling, then the slogan "reduce, reuse, recycle" would apply, right? Because I can absolutely reuse this. The street is empty and no nosy neighbors are watching from behind their curtains, so I drag the cardboard behind me all the way home.

Home is a generous word for a patch of dirt under a canoe, but I don't mind because today has been a good day. I have a job. I have a blanket. And now I even have a mattress. It takes some doing to free the industrial-sized staples that keep the box a box, but I get it flattened and shove it under the last canoe. Folding myself under, I test out my new setup and can't help but smile. I always wanted a canopy bed.

For better or worse, this is my home, and I can make it work. Removing a pen from my backpack, I scratch *Home Is Where the Heart Is* on the rim of the canoe above my head. This *is* where my heart is, isn't it? I close my eyes, waiting for exhaustion to sink me into sleep's embrace, but they snap open once again when I envision Nolan's questioning eyes asking me, *Who are you?*

The truth is not something I want to tell him.

10

My first paycheck is heavy in my pocket, weighted with relief.

I did it. I managed to survive two weeks without touching the remaining $3.75 in my account. I never want to eat another protein bar, but I imagine I'll be stuck with them for the time being. One paycheck does not provide much more of a safety net, and I need to be extremely careful, or I'll never be able to save enough for a place to live.

But right now, I'm proud of myself and might as well be filled with helium because I'm practically floating.

I'm so happy that I forget to avoid Lambert Avenue on my walk home from work. Passing the perfect window displays, I even start playing a game. *What if I could afford that outfit?* Or, *What if that came in my size?* It's a nice game, considering I can't afford anything, and nothing in these shops comes in my size, but the point of pretending is being able to forget about the pesky little details, like reality.

I'm standing in front of a window, staring at the display, wondering if I'd ever have the guts to wear a kelly green bikini. I'm not sure I could ever wear that, but I can't walk away from the display window. Lacie and Nolan are half a block away, walking toward me.

Lacie has her arm looped through Nolan's and they both hold some sort of drink. I'm still wearing my black work leggings, which are exactly the same as my black non-work leggings, but after my shift, I swapped my apron for my Bob Marley shirt. Gathering the ends of it, I tug it up, making a knot at my waist. Why did I just do that? I do not want Nolan to notice me. From what I've seen, I'm certain he's dating Lacie, and right now their arms are looped into a pretzel as they slowly walk down the sidewalk. So why did I just tie my shirt like this? To look less like a blob of black? To highlight the curves I hate?

They haven't seen me yet, so I take the opportunity to really stare at them. Nolan is wearing a pair of blue swim trunks and a white V-neck, and Lacie is wearing a pink polo and denim skirt. Nolan's height is exaggerated next to Lacie's petite frame. They look good together, like they could be on the cover of a magazine. The handsome giant with his Polly Pocket. It isn't fair of me to think of them like that, even if it is only inside my mind.

I will only ever be a blob of black. My fingers reach for the knot of fabric to undo what I just tied when Lacie spots me. She runs the half block, wrapping me in a hug, and Nolan has just caught up to us when Lacie asks, "Where have you been the past two weeks? Have you been avoiding us?"

I blink at her, unwilling to make my eyes meet Nolan's. "Yes," I answer.

There are a few seconds of silence, and then Lacie laughs her gravel road laugh. "You are so funny."

It's funny because it's true, but I don't say that. I've been avoiding the beach and this section of town, both of which seem to be where everyone congregates, tourist or not. But today I was happy. Today I hiked up my shirt and tied it in a knot when Nolan was half a block away. Today I am obviously having lapses in my judgment.

Lacie's arm threads back through the crook of Nolan's, and he takes a sip of what I can now see is boba tea. "What are you up to?" she asks.

"Oh, you know"—my hand flits toward the window next to me—"window shopping."

Lacie's and Nolan's eyes follow the motion of my hand which leaves the three of us staring at the green bikini and I want to melt into the sidewalk.

Lacie finishes a sip of her tea. "That would be killer on you. With your curves and skin tone—" She kisses her fingers.

I scrunch my face. Nobody has ever complimented me like that. Everyone I knew thought it was fine to call me Round Rindy. One foster dad even found it acceptable to say, "*If your hips get any wider, you'll be in the next county.*"

Never in my life has anyone told me, "*Hey, I bet that would look hot on you.*"

Nolan coughs and thumps his chest. When I glance in his direction, his face is the same shade of red that mine feels. But it's because a lump of tapioca went down the wrong pipe and not because he's visualizing me in that two-piece, right? His eyes catch mine and his cheeks burn a deeper shade. Oh great. It is because he's visualizing me in a bikini and it must be so repulsive it's making him choke.

At least that's a normal reaction for someone to have while thinking about the shape of my body.

Lacie slaps Nolan's back. "You okay?" Nolan nods and takes another sip, a risky move because Lacie says, "Seriously, you should buy that."

I spin away from the windows because I do not want to talk about the green bikini any longer. "So, where are you two headed?" I ask.

Nolan opens his mouth but Lacie cuts him off. "He bought me a peace offering. Or maybe he's bribing me because he knows my weakness." She raises her cup and sucks so hard on the straw that it's like she's doing fish lips.

"All I did was ask her to go camping this weekend," Nolan says.

"Exactly. Camping." Lacie shudders and raises her cup again. "This has to be a cup full of bribery because somehow I said yes." Her eyes pop open. "You should come. Please come. An entire weekend with him and Wick isn't the worst idea, but stuck in the woods with them? No. Not my thing. But if you come it would even the scales, and there'd be someone on my side."

On her side of what? Balancing the scales of male versus female? Camping lovers versus camping haters? It might shock her to discover I'm not on her side for that one.

"Oh, I don't know. I don't think I could." I twist the ends of my hair together. "I'd have to ..." I almost say *take time off work*, but catch myself, opting for a catch-all excuse. "You know, parents." I shrug because parents are a mystery and leave it at that.

"Sure. But at least ask," Lacie says, accepting my reason with ease, pulling out her phone as it chimes. "Oh shoot, I have to go. Poh Poh is going to kill me if I'm late again."

Before she leaves she unclips a pen hooked on the inside collar of her shirt, grabs my arm, and writes something on the back of my hand. "That's my number. Anytime. Especially if you need me to convince your parents that going camping with us is totally fine. I make very compelling PowerPoints."

Nolan gives Lacie a playful kick to her rear which stops her from talking. "Your grandmother is going to kill you, remember?" he says.

"Right. Yes." She walks away before yelling over her shoulder, "Catch you later."

My eyebrows scrunch together. "Lacie has a murderous grandmother?"

Nolan gestures to the Asian market two blocks down.

"Mrs. Lau, Lacie's grandmother, owns it, and Lacie works for her. But as you might have noticed Lacie can sometimes be a little—"

"Flighty?"

Nolan drains his tea and nods. We walk up the street, away from the market, and away from the bikini when Nolan says, "Could you be loved?"

My feet are suddenly glued to the sidewalk and my heart turns into a hammer. What on earth is he talking about? Love. What? My mouth gapes open and Nolan points at my shirt. "It's the only song of his I know."

I clamp my mouth shut. Of course. Marley. I can breathe again but my heart is still racing. "I'm not really knowledge-able when it comes to his music either," I say. "It was in the dollar bin at Goodwill." Even if Nolan is Beverly's son, plenty of people like thrifting, not just foster kids who end up homeless.

Nolan tosses his empty cup in the trash. "Haven't seen you around much. Been enjoying your vacation?"

Has he been hoping to run into me as much as I've been trying to avoid it? I pick at a patch of dry skin around my thumb. "Yes, it's been great so far. Everyone at the B Hive has been so kind." Nolan tilts his head to the side, and I want to jab my thumbs into my eyes. People on vacation do not talk about the employees at the hotel they are stay-ing at.

We walk a few more steps in silence. "What are you doing for the rest of the day?" he asks.

Basking in the fact that I am one paycheck closer to a place to live. "Not much. You?"

"I got my 4Runner back and I need to take it for a drive to make sure it's all systems go. Plus, I have to deliver a table."

We've reached the end of the sidewalk, and the end of another conversation with Nolan that I've enjoyed having. Except for the parts about the bikini, but technically he was a choking bystander in that conversation. "It was nice running into you," I say because I realize it's the truth.

If I enjoy talking with him so much, why have I been avoiding it? Because I'm a liar. Because he's Beverly's son. Because he's leaving at the end of the summer. Because I'm a big blob of black. And because he's dating Lacie. People that adorable belong together.

Nolan reaches out, touching my elbow. "Any chance you'd want to come with me?"

I freeze. JP's voice is loud in my ear, not Nolan's, and my head spins. Years ago, JP asked me this same question and it set off a chain of events that ruined any chance I had of finding a family.

"So, what do you say?" Nolan asks. "Up for a drive?"

My face must not give me away because Nolan is looking at me like everything is fine. Not realizing I'm locked inside a memory of meeting JP behind the middle school equipment shed—I trusted JP. He was the only one who knew I kept a book of matches stashed in my pocket, lighting one every day of May, trying to ignite a memory of the day I was born.

Sure, I had matches in my pocket, and yes, I lit one, but

burning the shed to the ground was not supposed to happen. JP was the only one who knew the truth, but he never said anything. He never said he was there with me, or that everything that happened was a colossal accident. He knew the truth and he let me burn.

I want to get as far away from these memories as possible, so I say, "Absolutely."

But as I walk next to Nolan, I'm still haunted by JP. It's this moment I revisit in my do-over game, wishing I never agreed to go with him. My life could have been so different. Finding a family that wants to adopt a thirteen-year-old girl who spent her entire life in the system isn't easy. It's like trying to get someone to pick the bruised apple sitting on top of all the crisp, perfect ones. But after the fire, finding a family that wanted to adopt me was impossible. Nobody wants a teen who plays with matches, so I got a one-way ticket to a group home.

It's only when we are at Nolan's car that I wonder if I'm doing it all over again. Am I trusting someone when I shouldn't? Is this another trap?

"Wait," I say, my voice catching on the edge of fear, and Nolan turns to me, his hand hovering next to the passenger door. "Shouldn't you ask Lacie?"

Nolan shakes his head. "Why would I need to check with Lacie?"

Because Lacie is stunning and tiny and fits next to you like a puzzle piece. Because both of you are beautiful. Because I'm a bruised apple. I roll the nylon straps of my backpack between my fingers. "She's your girlfriend, isn't she?"

Nolan's smile lights his eyes. "Lacie and I aren't together. She's my friend." There was a slight pause before he said friend like he wanted to use another word instead, but he opened the car door. "You've got me all to yourself." If Nolan were still drinking his tea he'd be choking again. "I don't mean you've got me. Or that you want to have me." He exhales so loudly it sounds like a groan, and he presses his forehead against the edge of the door. "Have you been to Crescent City yet?"

Something about watching Nolan squirm makes me smile. It unties the fear I've tangled around my ribs. "I haven't."

He lifts his head and smiles. "That's where I'm headed. A guy bought a table I made and after I drop it off, we could explore a little?"

With a nod, I accept another ride with Nolan.

11

"I can't believe you made this," I say, walking backward, carrying one end of the table Nolan is delivering.

"You can't believe it because I'm just some handsome beach bum?" His eyes give away nothing, but a whisper of a smile flirts at the edge of his lips.

I'm pretty sure I'm blushing. "You sound like Wick," I say.

The whisper of Nolan's smile blooms into a symphony that I could listen to on repeat every day. "Ouch, I deserved that."

"I mean, I have found you at the beach, sometimes without shoes, so maybe you are. But seriously this table is amazing," I say.

And it is. It's a hefty chunk of wood with raw edges, sanded and polished until it's as golden as honey. Three simple U-shaped iron legs are bolted into the bottom and if I had a house, this is exactly what I would want for a coffee table. My arms buckle and I almost drop my end of the table. The hope of having a place of my own, that I can fill with furniture I chose for myself, is a heavy load to carry alone. I want to set it down, but all I can let go of at the moment is the table Nolan made.

Nolan rings the bell and we wait, the table between us. When an older gentleman opens the door, I can't help but remember standing in front of a different older gentleman on a porch swept clean of sand much like this one. I shake away the memory of pounding my hand against the multicolored glass door as this man starts talking.

"Ah, Mr. Lambert, and his table," says the gentleman.

Nolan straightens his back, growing even taller. "Call me Nolan. Mr. Lambert is my father."

The gentleman nods, pushing the door wide open, allowing Nolan and myself and the table to enter. "Young men and their fathers," the gentleman says. "I remember saying that same thing many times over myself, and I didn't grow up in the shadow of a giant." Nolan coughs, his face turning red. I widen my eyes at Nolan in a universally silent, *Are you okay?* Nolan's nod is crisp and barely there as we follow the man through the entryway of his house to the living room, setting the table on a rug in front of a worn leather couch.

The man looks at it, then extends his hand to Nolan. "Fine work, Nolan Lambert."

The muscles in Nolan's jaw clench, but he shakes the

man's hand with a pristine smile. "If you want anything else, let me know, I'd be happy to make whatever you need."

Once we are outside Nolan releases a long breath and tips his face to the sky. Whatever bothered him inside the house starts to melt away. "All right. Where to next?" he asks.

I don't know where to go, and I don't want to spend energy pretending like I do. Nolan still has his face tilted skyward, eyes closed, recharging his soul in the sunlight. And because he feels the need to do that, and the fact that he wants to see the Pando as much as I do, I say, "Take me to your favorite view."

Nolan parks in a lot on the edge of town. "It's not my *favorite* view, but it's a good one, especially if—" He leaves the sentence unfinished, running to the railing and back. "Today's your lucky day."

"Why's that?"

"Two reasons." Nolan points to a food truck on the opposite end of the parking lot. "Elephant ears and low tide." My face scrunches and his hand flies to his chest. "Do not tell me you've never had an elephant ear."

Smiling I say, "Okay, I won't tell you that."

Grabbing my hand, he tugs me beside him to the food truck. "It's a good thing I found you when I did."

There is no line and we walk straight to the window.

"Two, please. No powdered sugar," Nolan orders. He's still holding my hand, and I don't want to breathe or blink or move in case he notices and lets go. But an invisible current of electricity connects our hands. Nolan must feel it too because he looks at the tangle of our knuckles.

When he lifts his face to mine, his smile is as dangerous as ever. "Huh," he says but he doesn't let go.

We stand at the window waiting for whatever in the world an elephant ear is, holding hands like it's no big deal. I dissect the word *huh* into a hundred different meanings, pulling petals off the situation. It means something. It means nothing. It means something. It means nothing.

I've landed on *it means something* when the woman inside the food truck sets two paper plates in front of us. I suppose the crispy circles of flat, fried bread look like the ear of an elephant, but it doesn't matter what it looks like, because it smells like cinnamon-sugar bliss and I can't wait to taste it. Our hands separate so we can grab the plates, and I'm left wishing these took longer to make.

I pluck another mental petal off of holding hands with Nolan. *It means nothing.*

Nolan rips a section of the bread and chews. "Lucky day reason number two is this way," he says.

Exiting the parking lot, we cross a street and walk down a path. I sample my first bite as we go and I was right, it's amazing. "I'm glad you found me when you did too," I say. Nolan is slightly in front of me, and he turns but before he can say anything I raise the paper plate in the air between us. "Because now I know what an elephant ear is."

Once we are on the beach, I see how close we are to a small island with a lighthouse nestled on it. There is a clear path from where we are walking leading up to the island and Nolan says, "At low tide, you can walk out to the island."

It only takes a few minutes to reach the island and there is nothing else there except a whitewashed stone building with a lighthouse column sprouting from the middle of its red roof. "People say it's haunted." Nolan tosses his empty plate in the trash and nods toward the building. "Want to go find out?"

My empty plate follows his into the bin. "Maybe after we see the island."

He nods. "Right. You'd pick being outside over discovering ghosts any day. I should have guessed."

We are met with a gust of wind as we round the building, nothing between us and the Pacific except for a few feet of rock. We both sit, our legs hanging over the edge, whitecaps churning under our feet.

"What did the guy you sold the table to mean when he said you grew up in the shadow of a giant?" That question has been nibbling at me since we left the house. It's none of my business. I don't want to open a door labeled *Personal Business* with Nolan because open doors are invitations for questions in return, but I'm curious, and thrown off-balance. I can still feel the shape of his hand in mine.

Nolan smooths a hand over the rocks beside his leg,

coming up with a small pebble that he rolls between his fingers. "My dad. He's a real estate legend. He either owns or has owned more along this coast than you can imagine. Some people make it a point to bring up my last name, to let me know they know, and it drives me crazy." He sighs and his back rounds down like he's tucking himself into a ball. "I'm not who my dad wants me to be." The pebble slips out of Nolan's hand, clinking once on the rock before disappearing into the depths of the ocean.

I wish I had a pebble to keep my hands busy with. "Who does he want you to be?"

"A replica of himself." Without a distraction, Nolan shoves his hands under his thighs. "I graduated last June, and all my dad has ever wanted is for me to follow his footsteps to UC Berkeley, and then join him at his company. He let me defer a year if I agreed to work for him." He shakes his head. "The year is almost up."

Nolan is a son anchored by the weight of his father, and I'm an abandoned daughter with no anchor at all. Neither of us knows where we belong. Maybe Nolan and I are not that different. "So, you're leaving instead," I say.

His head bobs up and down. "You like staying at the B Hive?" he asks.

The shift in our conversation is as sudden as the wind abruptly stopping and I almost forget I need to act like I stay in a room, not clean them. "It's amazing what your mom did to transform the place." Nolan looks at me and I shrug. "I read the brochure." There is a stack of them in the lobby; I figured I should know what they said and not just dust around them.

"Sure. The brochure. Does it mention how my dad bought the property for my mom as an apology for his affair?" My mouth swings open. "No? See," he says. "That's the thing with history, no one ever gets the telling of it quite right."

Beverly owns the B Hive because it was an apology for her husband's affair. Is that why she has very specific standards for it? I have no idea what to say and let the ocean crashing beneath our feet fill the silence. Nolan stands, so I follow him. We make our way around the other side of the island to where there is more of a shore, picking our way across tide pools. When I slip on a kelp-covered stone Nolan reaches out, grabbing me, keeping me from falling and we are suddenly very, very close.

"You're like a magnet," he says. "I keep finding my way to you." His skin is California-summer warm, and he slides his hand down my arm, reaching for my hand, threading his fingers through mine. I don't know who is steadying who anymore. "Is this okay?" he asks.

My eyes trace a line from our hands up to Nolan's face. "Huh," I say. My copy-paste of what Nolan said earlier makes him laugh and my stomach flips. Nothing will ever sound better than the ocean plus Nolan's laugh.

His forehead tips toward mine and the world shrinks away. "I've never met anyone like you." He squeezes my hand. "Who are you?"

My heart stops, and when it restarts it's thrashing against my ribs. This is my nightmare come true.

My entire body vibrates with each thud of my heart, but Nolan doesn't notice. "You have a very unfair advantage over me because I don't even know your full name." He says this as he reaches up to tuck a strand of hair behind my ear.

My name. My full name. Nolan is asking me to tell him something that constantly reminds me I was found missing. Part of me still is. I've always loved that my name is Rindy. I even love how Rindy Jane sounds together. The kicker is because there was no family lineage to file me under, I got stuck with Rindy Jane Doe. Try forgetting you were abandoned at birth with a name like that.

"Doe." My breath catches on the word. "Rindy Doe." It's all I can offer.

We walk closer to where the land meets the water before Nolan says, "Rindy Doe. I like the sound of that." My hand tightens in his and I tug him to a stop. "What's wrong?" he asks.

What's wrong is that I keep having to clip the truth into something easier to say, something easier to choose to be around. Because I know what the truth will do. No one has ever wanted the true version of me. I nod my head toward the waves slurping toward our toes. "I can't swim." It's the truth, but the fear of being swept out to sea is not why I clenched his hand.

The concern melts off his face and I wonder what he

thought I was going to admit. "How is that possible? Are your parents monsters?" he jokes.

He's joking, but maybe they are. I take two quick breaths. "Nope. Ghostwriters, remember." Banter is a much better situation than balancing on the tightrope strung between truth and lies. "Besides, Montana isn't exactly known for its oceanfront beaches."

"Oh yes, thank you for the real estate advice. I never get enough of that. Also. Lakes. There are plenty of amazing lakes in Montana." He bumps his side into mine, momentarily squishing our clamped hands between our legs. "We have a pool at the house. I could teach you." He pauses before adding, "On one condition."

I raise an eyebrow. "Condition?"

"Come camping with us this weekend, then I'll spend the rest of the summer teaching you how to swim."

I forgot all about his camping trip with Wick and Lacie. And now that I remember it, I also remember a certain green bikini. Nolan better not be thinking about that. He's not choking, but he is holding my hand, and I'm afraid my palm is suddenly very sweaty. I don't have a dangerous smile like he does, just an ordinary one, but when he sees my lips curve, he winks, and my stomach somersaults again.

Everything about this afternoon is outside the boundaries of my normal life. I have no idea how I'm going to ask for time off, or even if I can. I've only been an employee for two weeks, but for the second time today, I remind myself that pretending is all about not dealing with reality. I do not want to deal with my reality.

But I can't exactly ignore my reality when all I have is a canoe, a cardboard mattress, and a wool blanket. "I don't have any camping gear."

"Of course you don't. Who brings their camping gear on vacation? Unless you are camping." He squeezes my hand. "We have extra in the garage. I'll bring it."

Extra camping gear in the Lamberts' garage. It's probably stacked on a rack gathering dust next to Beverly's Tesla. I try to imagine Beverly camping, a bandana tied around her unwashed hair. The mental image makes me put my hand to my mouth, trying unsuccessfully to keep my laugh inside.

"Can I take that as a yes?" Nolan's eyes are the ocean, and I start to sink because I do not know how to swim.

But if I go camping, Nolan said he would teach me so I say, "You've got yourself a deal."

12

I'm giving myself an ulcer.

Driving home from the lighthouse, Nolan told me he needed go to Sacramento for the rest of the week with his dad to *close a deal*. Then he had asked for my phone number. I told him a story that my parents and I are having a technology free summer. I let him believe it was immersive research for their next project. He was impressed and I felt sick for not telling him the truth.

Lies. Lies. Lies.

They are eating me from the inside, shredding my stomach into pieces, and I lean my head against my locker at the end of my shift. This pain could also be from a serious lack of fresh fruit and too many protein bars. Either way, my life is trying to kill me.

I had the entire week to ask for time off, but I never did. How could I? It's only my third week of work. Besides, what am I supposed to do—walk into Beverly's office and say, "Hi, I was hoping I could have a few days off so I can go camping with your son."

That would not go over very well.

I *want* to go camping with Nolan, but I *need* to keep this job.

Nolan is going to be at Center Park, conveniently named because it's in the center of Tinlee Bay, waiting for me in exactly one hour, and all I'm doing is standing with my forehead pressed against my locker. It was nice pretending that time with Nolan meant something, but I can't go. Not when my job is on the line. I have no idea what Nolan will do when I don't show up. There's no way I'll ever be able to explain my way out of agreeing to go and then ghosting him.

"Well, that's one way to end your day." Mina's voice startles me, but I don't move. Her tone softens. "Did something happen? Was it the guy in one-seventeen?"

That makes me lift my head and offer a halfhearted smile. The man in room one-seventeen has been pestering both of us with what he calls emergencies all week. First, he couldn't find his room slippers. Then there were two packets of Earl Gray at his coffee station instead of one plus English Breakfast. Today he insisted that all his hand towels were missing.

But when Mina sees my face she says, "Oh no. I've seen those eyes before. What's his name?"

"Nolan." I say it without thinking because his name has been on the tip of my tongue all day.

Mina's eyebrows practically shoot to her hairline. "Nolan Lambert?" she clarifies, and I nod.

And since I've already opened this particular can of worms, I add, "He invited me to go camping this weekend."

Mina steps forward, touching the back of her hand to my forehead. "You're burning up."

I'm confused by this because of all the things I am right now, I know I'm not sick. Unless I really do have scurvy.

Mina doesn't offer an explanation, she just holds her hand to her ear as if it were a phone. "Hello? Speak up. Is that you, Rindy? You sound like death warmed over. Uh-huh, okay, too sick to come to work? Fever, gosh, that bad?" She holds one finger up in my direction to shush any protest I could offer in my confusion, nodding her head, really selling this make-believe conversation. "You'll be completely recovered by rise-and-shine-o'clock Monday morning? I understand."

She hangs up by putting her hand in her apron pocket and I stumble over my words. "What are you doing?"

"Nolan is one of the good ones, and youth is a short-lived victory. Plus"—she pulls me away from my locker to the computer, tapping keys to wake it up—"have you seen the bookings for this weekend?" I check the screen. There are more vacancies than reserved rooms. "Happens sometimes, an unpredictable lull."

Mina might as well be speaking a different language. "What are you saying? What about Beverly?"

"I'm saying I can manage for two days without you.

Beverly and I have been friends forever, don't worry about her." Mina winks, and I try to hide my shock. Is she serious? Mina is as sweet as a tangerine, and Beverly is a stalk of celery. How are they best friends? "Hector will get jealous of you hanging out with someone else," Mina adds, "but what can be done?"

She taps a few more keys, bringing up a new screen. "I'm also saying that next weekend we have a bachelorette party, and the following weekend there is a family reunion, and the following weekend ..."

Mina doesn't finish but I understand. She is giving me the weekend off while letting me know this is a one-time occurrence.

"I don't know what to say."

"Then don't say anything," she laughs, "and get your booty out of here before I change my mind."

I'm the first one to arrive at the park, which gives me a chance to stop breathing like I sprinted the entire way. I can't believe this is happening. I'm really going to do this. I've wondered what seeing Nolan would be like after our afternoon on the island followed by complete radio silence. Will he act as if nothing happened? Act as if something happened? Will he try to explain it away by saying something like, "So, about the other day."

It meant something. It meant nothing. It meant something. It meant nothing.

Nolan drives up as I'm ripping more mental petals off an imaginary flower. He leaves the car running, walking straight to me, brushing a finger along my jaw, making my skin feel like the Fourth of July.

"I missed you," he says.

Spending time together means something. I try to keep my voice level. "How was your trip?"

He rolls his eyes. "Do they teach people how to schmooze in business school? It has to be a mandatory class. That and golf. Because that's all it was."

Only a few inches separate us, but the air is charged, and he curls his pinky around mine, linking us together. Wick emerges from somewhere. Did he arrive with Nolan? For all I know he sprang up from behind a shrub. I back up but Nolan moves with me, our fingers still locked like a chain.

"Hey, Wick," I say.

Wick gives a raised eyebrow and chin tilt combination as his hello, keeping his eyes on his phone. "Lacie just texted," he says. "We need to go pick her up. Something about having too much to carry."

The four of us are packed into Nolan's car, stuffed around Lacie's multitude of bags. She insisted they are in case of an emergency, but I can't imagine what camping emergency would require this much stuff. She sits in the front next to Nolan, Wick sits behind her, and I'm behind Nolan. The longer north we drive, the more it feels as if we are retracing our steps to Crescent City and the afternoon we spent together. I've caught Nolan's eye several times in the rearview mirror. Is he thinking about spending time at the lighthouse too?

We veer away from the ocean and the farther inland we drive, the larger the trees grow. They loom over us, silent guardians of the passage of time. I have loved discovering the ocean, loved standing at its edge, and watching its moods shift and surge. The way the water stretches endlessly away from the shore is a marvel. But the swaying limbs in the forest match the tempo of my pulse. If I was attached to a monitor that prints out your heartbeat, mine would look like pine trees all in a row.

Not for the first time I wonder if I'd feel this way about the forest had I grown up someplace else. Did it take being abandoned in the middle of Montana to feel at home inside a grove of trees? Or was that always hardwired inside my heart?

Nolan navigates a road that is little more than a path, then pulls to a stop in a clearing with two large, downed trees and we all tumble out. This isn't a campground at a state park, it's just a patch of earth, and I'm guessing we are the only ones around for miles.

I spin a circle with my head to the sky, enjoying how the

trees blur at the edge of my vision and when I stop, Nolan is watching me.

"Do you like it?" he asks.

My stomach no longer aches like it did at the end of my shift. I am breathless and very alive. "I love it," I say.

Lacie and Wick round the car and we're all grouped together. Wick twists his back, making bones click and Lacie asks, "So, where's the bathroom?"

At the back of his car, Nolan fishes out a roll of toilet paper, tossing it to Lacie. "Pick a tree," he tells her.

If looks could kill, Nolan would be dead on the ground. "No." Lacie squeezes the toilet paper between her hands like a vice. "I'm not playing games. I agreed to come camping. I did not agree to mark my territory like a beast."

It's not Lacie's fault. There is camping, and then there is *camping*. I don't want to laugh and have Lacie assume I'm laughing at her, so I just tug the sleeve of her shirt and say, "Come with me."

We're a few steps away and Lacie yells, "You'll pay for this, Lambert." I don't look back, but I wonder if Nolan clenched his jaw. Does Lacie know how much that bothers him? I can't be the only person he's told.

By the time Lacie and I return, the flat rectangle attached to the top of Nolan's 4Runner has transformed into a rooftop tent, a ladder clipped to the side.

"Whoa, that was fast." I expected yards of nylon and poles strewn on the ground, an argument brewing between the boys about how exactly the tent should be assembled.

"Pretty sweet, isn't it? It's how Lamby will survive when he strikes out on his own," says Wick.

"This is your plan?" I ask Nolan as he circles rocks, making a fire pit.

He straightens up. "*Plan* makes it sound like I have everything figured out, which I don't. But, yes, this is the general idea. Camping. Back roads. Connecting with other woodworkers. Figuring out who I am away from—"

"Us," Lacie says, shoving the squished roll of toilet paper into Nolan's chest.

"No. Him," Nolan says, and we all know who he means.

Wick lightens the mood. "And bathrooms. You can figure out who you are far, far away from those."

The sun is already dipping in the sky and with the trees so thick, the light will go faster than we expect. "Wick, be useful and come help me gather firewood," I say.

He bounds over to me, and I want to throw a stick and watch him fetch. As we wander away Wick asks, "If you could be any animal, what animal would you be?"

"I have no idea," I say.

I'm probably a turtle because I sleep under the shell of a canoe. I stop walking. Actually, if any of us is a turtle, it would be Nolan with a tent attached to his car, ready to leave. My stomach clenches and it's not from lack of fruit or fear of asking for time off. What will life in Tinlee Bay be like without Nolan? I swallow. "You'd be a capybara."

Wick snaps a branch off a tree, then another one. "What the heck is that?"

I scuff away a pile of pine needles looking for sticks. "A South American rodent. One of my teachers last year was obsessed with them. They are super social and sometimes get called nature's ottoman because apparently, they don't mind giving other animals a ride."

"Uber rats," Wick laughs. "Leave it to Mother Nature to beat us to the punch. But if you wanted to sit on my lap, all you had to do was ask." Wick's smile is the deep end of the pool, and he knows it. He turns toward the campsite, yelling, "Rindy thinks I'm a rat!" Then he snaps another branch off a tree. "Why am I the only one collecting firewood?" he asks.

I'm about to grab a few twigs off the ground when I stop. From my bent-in-half position Wick is upside-down as he snaps yet another branch off a tree. "Are you being serious?"

Wick fills his cheeks with air. "Does anyone ever call you Rinds?" I shake my head. "Too bad, I like the sound of it. Anyway, by now you should know I am *always* serious."

I shake my head again, but also smile. "Well, I hate to break it to you, but you're not gathering firewood." His eyebrows scrunch together, and I swat the branches out of his arms, letting them fall to the ground. "What you keep breaking off is fresh wood. It's too wet to burn." I lift the dried piece I was about to grab a second ago. "Dead and dry, that's what you need."

He salutes. "Wood that represents Lamby's love life. Check."

I've already bent to pick up another piece of wood and

hope I managed to hide my face before Wick noticed the flush rise to my cheeks.

We return to the clearing, our arms filled with wood. "I learned two things," Wick announces. "Firewood needs to be dead just like your heart, Lamby. And. Rindy would be the only one of us to survive the zombie apocalypse." Wick dumps his stack of wood to the ground, reaching over to the top of my stack, holding up my discovery. It's a large, ruffled mushroom that looks more like a piece of orange coral than your typical mushroom. "Go ahead, guess what this is," Wick asks.

"Something disgusting," Lacie offers, and Nolan shakes his head.

I've stacked the wood Wick and I collected into a pile. "See," says Wick, "Rindy would survive. The rest of us—" He slices a line across his throat. "This is"—Wick turns to me —"what did you call it?"

"Chicken of the woods. It's a mushroom."

Nolan looks at me with the same I-can't-believe-you-also-want-to-go-to-the-Pando expression. What would it be like to forage with him? To set up this tent wherever we wanted and wander the woods together? Nolan and I, the only people for miles. My cheeks flush again.

"A freaking mushroom," Wick exclaims.

"Please tell me we're not eating that," Lacie groans. "Peeing in a hole I dug in the dirt is enough of an adventure for one day without eating something you scraped off the ground."

Lacie shudders but Wick wraps his arms around her, swinging her off the ground. "Of course we are! We're out here surviving the zombie apocalypse."

She smiles, finally deciding to play along. "Fine. When the zombies come, Rindy will feed us. Nolan can build us a house, and I'll fashion leaves into stunning ensembles." She turns to Wick. "What will you do?"

He kisses her cheek. "So glad you asked. I'll repopulate the Earth with you."

"You wish." Lacie shoves Wick away, but not without a deep-end-of-the-pool smile of her own. I wait for Wick to bow or backflip or something else Wick-like, but he just stands there looking very pleased with himself.

The fire Nolan started is nice and hot when I cook the mushroom and Wick declares we'll have a taste test. From his backpack, he pulls out a Tupperware container stuffed with finger-licking chicken. "What?" He shrugs. As if bringing fast food to a campout is normal. Maybe it is. I only ever went camping with Sylvia and she is not your typical camper. I owe my foraging knowledge to her.

We eat all the chicken and Lacie admits the tiny sliver of the mushroom she allowed past her lips tasted better than it looked.

We all lean against the two downed trees, enjoying the warmth of the fire and our very full stomachs when Wick asks, "Favorite vampire?"

My head is tipped to the sky, attempting to decipher the Morse Code dots and dashes the stars make across the velvet.

"Anyone but Edward Cullen," I say, and it instantly falls silent. Even the forest stops breathing as six eyes are fixed on me.

"How many years did you dress up as Edward for Halloween?" Nolan asks Wick.

Wick tosses a twig into the fire, sending sparks scattering in every direction. "I blame those years on my sisters." He looks at me. "For the record, I have six. All older. All with a very strong Twilight obsession."

Lacie laughs so hard she struggles to get her words out. "Don't blame them. You were so invested. I have never seen another person more invested than you."

Wick clears his throat, throwing another stick into the fire. "My therapist says it's perfectly fine for me to blame others."

Before Wick can come up with another question Nolan asks, "Favorite tree?"

I'm no longer watching the brilliant dashes of the stars blink across the sky. I'm watching these people be friends. "Ponderosa," I answer.

Nolan answers his own question with, "Hickory. Unless we are purely going for show, then Jacaranda."

Wick scratches his head, leaning closer to Lacie. "People have favorite trees?"

"Favorite cloud," I ask, tucking my feet under my legs, giving my own answer. "Mammatus."

A smile spreads across Nolan's face. It really should come with a warning sign. "Ominous," he says.

I shake my head. "Not an official classification."

He cocks an eyebrow, his lip curling with it. "Huh."

Nolan is across the fire from me, his face covered in shadow and flame, far enough away that I shouldn't feel his words, but I do. The word races down my spine and I remember his finger locking around mine. *Huh.* It means something. It means nothing. It means something. It means nothing.

Wick nudges Lacie's arm. "What's happening? Are we stuck inside a nature show? How do we change the channel?" he asks.

Lacie pats Wick's arm and asks, "Favorite place? Mine is home." She leans over Wick, so I can see her face. "It's just me, my mom, and Poh Poh. I don't know who my dad is." A curse slips past her lips.

"Don't call him that." Nolan cringes. "Besides. Fathers can be overrated."

My mouth is wide open. Not only because I'm not the only one at this fire who doesn't know who their father is, but because if it were just the three of them out here on this trip they wouldn't need to keep providing these little asterisks of clarification regarding their lives. These are purely for my benefit. They feel like an invitation on expensive paper, sealed with wax.

Wick pushes the tip of a stick into the fire. "In case anyone was wondering, my favorite place is a tie between the balcony at the Langston Theater and the walk-in cooler at Costco." Lacie makes a strange squawking sound somewhere between a laugh and a cry. "What? Is it a crime to have two favorites?" Wick asks, leaning his head on Lacie's shoulder.

Coming to Tinlee Bay was supposed to check a lot of things off my list. Finding people who mean so much to me is more than I dreamed. I am desperate to make it on my own because everyone failed me. My parents. The system. Everyone. I need to prove to myself that I am capable and that I am not a waste of space or resources. But wanting to claw myself out of this hole all by myself does not mean I want to spend my life alone.

"I used to go camping with my neighbor, and if anyone is going to survive the zombies, it'll be Sylvia." I pick apart the leaf I've been twirling by its stem. "One time we were out who-knows-where and I asked her if she always knew she belonged inside the forest." I can't keep the smile off my face at the memory of Sylvia securing her hammock between two trees before throwing herself into it. No one would ever guess she was almost eighty years old. I've turned the leaf into a pile of dust and sweep it from my legs. "Anyway, she told me there's a section of land on the trail linking Hub and Hazel Lakes where her pulse slows, and she knows she's home." This entire time I've kept my eyes down, looking anywhere but at Nolan. I finally lift my eyes to his. "She said everyone has a piece of earth that only belongs to them, you just have to find it."

It's the most truth I've offered, and saying it aloud makes me feel like I've finally come up for air.

Nolan won't take his eyes off mine. He's not even blinking. "And have you? Have you found the place where you belong?"

Everything I could say is trapped inside my heart, locked behind lips that can't make a sound. I simply shake my head.

He nods as if he understands. He has to. He's the one preparing to set off to figure out who he is and find where he belongs, somewhere no one knows his last name. "Well, this place is climbing the charts. I also currently would have to add tide pools and lighthouses to the list."

Every time I pull a petal off spending time with Nolan and the things he says, I get more confused about which way I want them to fall. If it means something, I'll have to tell him the truth. And if it means nothing, I'll have to hide my heart. Both are costly and make my chest pound for different reasons.

The fire is a pile of embers when Lacie asks, "Do I also have to sleep behind a tree?"

Nolan pushes himself to stand, offering a hand to Lacie. "It might be a squish, but we can all fit in the tent," he says.

Lacie grabs Nolan's hand with a yawn then stretches her arms over her head. "Finally, something that sounds decent."

Wick stands, offering me his hand. "Allow me."

But I shock everyone when I say, "Thanks, but I'd rather sleep out here."

It's not that I'm against squishing in the tent with these people who are becoming my friends. What I have to stay away from is the mattress. Sleeping on the ground night after night after night comes with serious drawbacks, but I've grown numb to it in every way possible. I'm worried if I allow myself to sink into something soft, the ground will be unbearable to return to.

Wick and Nolan exchange a glance I can't read. "Flip ya for it," Wick says.

Nolan shakes his head. "Toss me the stuff I left in the tent and keep your hands off Lacie."

"So. Many. Rules." Wick stomps up the ladder. Then two sleeping bags fly out of the tent followed by two pillows and the sound of a zipper slowly being pulled fills the night.

Lacie's voice is muffled from inside the tent. "You are such a child," she says.

Then Wick unzips the tent, poking his head out the flap, pressing his hand to his lips, and flings a series of air kisses in our direction. "Love you, good night."

Nolan laughs, collecting the strewn belongings, then jabs the embers with a stick before adding more logs that burn with a satisfying crackle.

He hands me a sleeping bag that I remove from the stuff sack, shimmying into it, falling to the ground in an attempt to sit.

Before Nolan does the same, he asks, "Is it okay if I stay out here with you?"

With me. Every single petal blows off the flower in my mind.

Once again, the world shrinks to only Nolan and me.

Nolan tips his head to the tent perched on his truck. "Afraid of heights?"

I shake my head. I'm not afraid of that, but there are several other things I'm afraid of. Like, what would Nolan think of me if he knew I'm sleeping on the ground because I was scammed out of a place to live, and that I have no family because no one has ever wanted to keep me?

Nolan's next words vibrate through the empty night. "I was hoping we could talk."

My back stiffens. It sounds a lot like *one day this will all make sense*, and despite the fact that I feel happy, despite being next to Nolan, I know right here, in the middle of nowhere, is where I'll be crushed.

"My mom's hosting a fundraiser and she's been on my case because I'm leaving and throwing away my future. You get the idea." Nolan inchworms his way closer until there is no space between the sides of our cocooned bodies. "But if you came with me, I'd be able to survive attending."

My mouth is instantly dry. The night is a ceiling above us, the rustle of branches is all around us, and the snap and hiss from the flames keep us company. It's perfect, and I was not expecting him to say this. I was expecting disappointment. "Are you asking me—"

"On a date. Yes." Nolan shifts so I can see his face. "Preferably not just one."

Not just one date. This isn't a "*Hey, you seem fun, we could survive a horrible evening together*" ask. This isn't *one day this will all make sense*. This is *Something*. It is also a date that involves an event Beverly is hosting. What are the chances she wouldn't go to her own event? I huff out a breath so hard the hair by my cheek flutters. I'm still pretending the details of my life don't matter so I stop thinking about Beverly.

"I'd like that." My voice sounds as wispy as the smoke arching away from the flames, and I lay my head on Nolan's shoulder.

Above me, the stars still flicker messages I can't read. Maybe they are warning signs telling me that agreeing to go with Nolan is a horrible idea. I close my eyes. I'm exhausted and I'm tucked inside a cocoon next to a boy who wants to spend time with me. I know I'm slipping into more dangerous territory than just falling asleep. Whatever this feeling is that is growing inside my heart, it is expanding and very hard to ignore. I'm not sure I'd be able to stop it, even if I tried.

13

I wake up to a hiss in my ear. Imagining a snake, my body coils in a ball, but a hand clamps my shoulder and Lacie whispers, "Help me find one of my bags."

On my back, I'm breathing heavily, trying to calm down from my startling wake-up. My head is on Nolan's arm, and I try not to smile as I wriggle my way out of my cocoon, attempting not to wake him. It's like playing Twister and I despise that game, but this version is a different story. I could get used to any version of any game that involved being next to Nolan.

"Interesting," Lacie says, her voice still a clenched hiss. "I need details." She waves her hand from where I now stand next to her, to where Nolan sleeps on the ground. "But first, I seriously need you to help me find my medicine."

At that, my heart stops. Images of an EpiPen or an insulin-filled syringe flood my mind, and a hot wave of pins presses into my back. I don't like needles, and I do not know how to help with an emergency like that. My face betrays me because Lacie adds, "I woke up with the world's worst cramps."

Once again, I take a few breaths to allow my heart to stop jackhammering my ribs before following Lacie to the 4Runner. We've searched every one of the bags Lacie brought without a sign of anything resembling Tylenol. I'm on a second pass through the bags now, and Lacie is curled in a ball on the seat next to me, one hand on her forehead, the other on her abdomen. "I'm getting a migraine," she says.

I had a headache on my second or third day at the Hive and no amount of water or free cups of coffee from the break room next to the kitchen put a dent in it. I finally caved and asked Mina if she had something. She did and now there's an entire bottle of Tylenol on the shelf above the computer in the storage room for anyone to use. It's not for anyone. She put the medicine there for me. It's shocking how many times guilt and gratitude feel like the same emotion. Like one of those optical illusions where you look at a sketch and see a beautiful young woman, but then your eyes shift, and the young woman is a witch. So much of my life feels like that. Depending on the day I either feel thankful for Mina's unquestionable kindness, or guilty that I'm dependent on it.

I rest my hand on Lacie's shoulder, wishing I had something to give her. We're supposed to stay here all day and break camp first thing tomorrow morning. Out here there is no easy way to run to the store. We're so far into the woods that by the time we make it back to the highway, we might as well just keep driving to Tinlee Bay.

Leaving Lacie on the seat, I walk to where Nolan still sleeps. Before I wake him, I take a moment to study his face. He looks softer, more childlike, in his sleep even though stubble covers his cheeks and chin. Crouching down, my hand hovers over his face before I allow myself to run the tips of my fingers over his skin. He's warm and I'd like to crawl back into my sleeping bag. He shivers at my touch, his eyes fluttering open.

He offers me a sleepy smile. "Hey." His voice is sandpaper, and he clears his throat. Noticing I've already emerged from my cocoon, he sits up. "Everything okay?"

"Lacie's sick," I say.

As we reach his truck, Lacie tumbles out the door, landing on all fours, starting to vomit. Nolan rushes to her, holding her hair back, telling her it's going to be okay. I stand and watch. When it's over, Nolan kicks dirt over her mess and scoops Lacie up, leaning into the vehicle and depositing her on the bench seat. Once again, I feel like an intruder in their lives. They have an entire lifetime of friendship that I don't belong in.

I want to stop feeling like I'm trespassing in my own life.

I turn away from whatever hushed words Nolan offers Lacie, returning to the sleeping bags, zipping them and stuffing them into their sacks.

I should know better than to pretend as if I could slip inside the pockets of these friends. I know my place, and it's always on the fringe. Nolan's mom is my boss, and I don't belong here with them. As I settle into my own pity party, Nolan's arms wrap around me, his chin resting on my shoulder.

"That wasn't the wake-up I was expecting." His voice is no longer sleep-deep. "Did you sleep okay?" I lift my hands, holding on to his arms like they are an anchor, and it makes me laugh because it probably looks like he's choking me and I'm trying to escape. "What's so funny?" he asks.

I shrug. "Nothing. And yes, I slept fine, thanks." The first night in Tinlee Bay was the best night of sleep I've had since arriving. My body was too exhausted to care about the cold hard ground. Since then, even with the help of my cardboard mattress, I wake up at least once with a numb limb. But last night I slept like a baby, that is until Lacie scared me awake.

Nolan spins me so I'm facing him, never letting me out of his embrace. "You are a wonder, Rindy Doe. Did you know that?"

A wonder. Another thing I've never been called. Or ever thought about myself. Before tears start to sting my eyes, I press my head into the soft spot next to Nolan's shoulder. He smells like campfire and sleep, and the word *home* buzzes to life in my heart. My head jerks back as if I licked a battery. Nolan is not my home, he can't be. Home is a roof, wall-to-wall carpet, and security. Yet Nolan is a mountain and I've found shelter next to him. I've never felt so comfortable with anyone in my life. Still, people cannot be home, because people are not permanent.

"So, what's the plan?" I ask, keeping my emotions to myself.

"I'll wake up Wick and we'll head home. But first—" Nolan turns me around so we are side by side, his left arm over my shoulder. In front of us is a gap between the endless rows of trees, too narrow to be a clearing but wide enough to offer a window to the sky. The heavens are an indigo ombre, lighter at the bottom, darker at the top. The kind of predawn announcement that lets you know once the sun makes an appearance, it's going to be a glorious day. Even though we are breaking camp, when I wish we could stay, I have a feeling it's going to be a good day.

Turns out Nolan's rooftop tent is just as fast to pack away as it was to assemble, and as the sun melts away the last of the indigo, we're pulling away. I twist my head, and the two fallen trees we reclined against grow smaller until I can no longer see them. When I finally look out the windshield to where we are going instead of where we were, Nolan squeezes my hand. "Next time," he says.

He doesn't offer anything else but my brain races to fill in a few possibilities. Next time we'll stay longer. Next time it will be the two of us. Next time seems self-explanatory and my heart grows wings.

Lacie is still balled in the back seat, her head resting in Wick's lap. "I don't understand how in eighty-nine bags of stuff you didn't bring any Tylenol," Wick says.

"I did," Lacie moans. "I put my zippy panda pouch in my pink JanSport." Another moan. "At least I thought I did. And if you crack a joke about cramps, I'll kill you. Actually—" She retrieves her phone from under her leg, tapping it to life, tilting it toward her mouth before saying, "Amazon." A slight pause as the page opens, then, "Taser." Wick makes a sound in protest, but Lacie shushes him. "I can buy a hot pink one for twenty bucks."

Wick raises his voice. "Siri, turn off the phone."

Nolan lets out a rumble of a laugh and I can't help but curve my lips around the sound. "Lacie, before you buy it, I know for a fact Percy has one of those period pain simulator devices," Nolan says.

Wick sounds like a cat who got his tail closed in a door. "What? No."

"Are you serious?" Lacie asks. "I'm texting her right now. I am so going to torture you."

There's a scuffle and Wick snatches Lacie's phone out of her hand and she says, "Give that back."

I don't know who Percy is, and asking is another reminder that I don't belong in the folds of their lives. But I ask anyway, "Who's Percy?"

Nolan takes his eyes off the road and winks at me. I'm not prepared for it, or used to it, and it gives me the same I-licked-a-battery feeling. "One of Wick's Twilight-loving sisters."

"Apparently the evil one if she owns a torture device," Wick says. It's quiet for a moment before he asks, "How exactly do you know she has one?"

"It was her final project for Allsbrook's class," Nolan

answers, then tilts his head in my direction. "Percy and I graduated together. Lacie and Wick are stuck in high school purgatory for another year before they'll be set free to terrorize society."

I offer my own asterisk of explanation to my life. "I graduated a few weeks ago."

Lacie sighs. Or moans. It's hard to tell. "Stop reminding me that I have an entire year. On my own. Without you around to keep me sane," she says.

"So, what, I'm just chopped liver over here?" Wick asks.

Lacie snorts. "You will be after my taser arrives."

Wick whimpers while the rest of us laugh. I rest my head on the window, and even though I wish I was resting it on the trunk of one of the trees we left behind, this isn't such a bad ending to our camping trip.

14

Lacie's house is a block off Lambert Avenue, and I bet you can see the ocean from the second-story windows. Her bedroom must be up there and I bet she slides the glass up, breathing in the brine every morning. But maybe after a lifetime of living next to the sea, you stop drinking it in. Which seems like a waste. I hope I never get over the taste of salt in the air.

Lacie leans against Nolan as he walks her to the front door. Wick and I are behind them, loaded down with her bags. As Lacie pulls a key from her pocket, Wick looks at me.

"Maybe you're an alpaca?" He squints. "You always have that backpack of yours with you." He tilts his head as if imagining me as a sure-footed creature scaling the Andes. "Nope. That's not it. Don't worry, your inner animal will be revealed at the proper time."

I should save him some time. Tell him to go home and search the internet for animals that pretend to be other animals in order to fit in. Maybe I'm an opossum—playing dead in order to survive.

Lacie pushes the door open. "Mom? Poh Poh?" Her words echo back unanswered, and she turns to Nolan. "What time is it?" Nolan tells her it's a little after eleven and Lacie sighs while lowering herself onto the couch. "Poh Poh's at the market and Mom should be back at two. You can go, I'll be fine. Just bring me some Tylenol. And water. And maybe a trash can."

"No. We can stay," Nolan says. Lacie takes up two of the couch cushions and Nolan sits on the third, his hand on her foot.

Her eyes close as she slowly moves her hand over her body. "Like this is the Saturday you had planned."

Normally the sight of them so cozy would make me want to find some other place to look. But the memory of a campfire and a cocoon is still fresh in my mind.

"Well, no, but whatever, that doesn't matter. It wouldn't be right to leave you like this," Nolan says.

Nolan's words slice my heart in half. Lacie shouldn't be left alone, abandoned, or forced to fend for herself while she's feeling unwell. It's the right thing to do and it hurts. I've lost countless hours of sleep wishing my mom would have felt the same way about me. I've imagined all the reasons she would leave a baby in a box at a gas station, and none of them are pretty. Did she want to? Did she feel trapped? Did she think it was the only option? Rationally I know wanting to abandon your own child, and feeling desperate or being forced into the decision, are all wildly different reasons, but they all feel the same.

I needed someone to take care of me, and no one did the right thing. I'd never want anyone to feel the way I did, even if it is just a horrible case of cramps.

Taking a step away from Nolan and Lacie, I try to back out of the room, only to accidentally collide with an armchair, falling ungracefully into it. Asking as I recover, "Is the medicine in the bathroom cabinet?" I jab my thumb down the hall and Nolan lifts his eyes to mine with another wink I'm unprepared for.

"First door on the left," he says.

In sixth grade, we took a field trip to Glacier National Park, and not far from the park's entrance is a house of mystery. Of course, the school thought it would be a good idea to stop and eat our packed lunches there. Apparently, there's some kind of vortex, and in the 1970s someone built a shack in the middle of it. Everything is crooked, nothing is level. You can't stand up straight in the room, and what should be a simple walk across the floor feels like you'll tip off the edge of the world. It's exactly how I feel walking down the hall in Lacie's house.

The rules of physics do not apply inside a vortex. But they do in my life. Rule number three clearly states that with every action in nature, there is an equal and opposite reaction. I'm living proof it's true. Lacie doesn't know who her father is, and neither do I, but her life is so normal. She has a house, a mom, a grandmother, and friends who would do anything for her.

Things I can only dream of.

The bathroom is painted a nice beach house blue above the white wainscoting, and I lean my head above the light switch. The cool wall is a comfort, but I must stay like this longer than I realize because Nolan appears at my side. "You okay?" he asks.

My eyes snap open and I lift my head. "Yep. Fine." I smile but it feels as if my lips are made from cardboard.

Nolan's hand gently curls around my shoulder and there's a small crease between his eyes. "You sure? You could tell me even if you weren't."

He says that, but I'm not sure I believe him. Even if I wanted to open my mouth and spew my life story right here onto the immaculate tiles at his feet, nothing good would come of it. I know firsthand what people do when they know the truth about me, they pass me off to someone else, and I'd rather not experience that with Nolan. "Just tired I guess," I say, attempting a less cardboard smile this time.

Nolan pulls me into his chest, wrapping me in a hug. It eases some of the tension across my shoulders, but my heart is still constricted. I'm afraid to relax in his hug. I've been invited to step across welcome mats before, but sooner or later everyone realizes the mistake they made by inviting me in. They see the mistake I am, it's what always happens.

Pushing myself out of his arms, I say, "I should get the medicine to Lacie."

Not even ten minutes after Lacie swallows the pills, she falls asleep.

Wick is now the one sitting on the third cushion. "You guys should jet. No reason the three of us need to stay and watch her sleep. I'll wait until Jade gets home."

Nolan raises an eyebrow, unsure.

"I won't do anything stupid," Wick says.

Nolan looks at Wick for a very long time, then over at me, then back to Wick who lifts a three-finger salute. "On my honor," Wick promises.

Nolan scrubs his hands over his face and through his hair, making brown tufts stick out in all directions. "Fine, but call if you need me."

Wick tugs the knit blanket off the top of the couch, draping it over Lacie and tucking his feet under it as well. "Okay, Mom."

Nolan rolls his eyes and hooks his arm around my shoulder as we exit the house. Outside we both take a breath of the sea-clean air. Maybe no one ever gets used to drinking it in.

After a minute Nolan says, "I have the perfect idea."

I'm not sure I would call bowling the perfect idea, but Strike the High Note isn't just any bowling alley. It's also a pizza restaurant with a karaoke corner, and apparently, we've beaten the rush because the parking lot is mostly empty. Nolan opens my door, but before I get out, I admit, "We were supposed to be camping all weekend; I don't have my wallet with me."

"Excellent." He holds his hand out. "Date number one, it's official."

Who could resist his smile? And why does he keep aiming it at me? I feel like someone off to the side is going to yell *cut*, the scene will end, and Nolan will walk away, relieved he can stop acting. But he's there, in front of me, offering his hand and I take it.

I find a purple eight-pound ball and hold it under my chin, biting my lip. "Maybe you shouldn't watch me." Nolan shakes his head, his brown hair flopping from side to side. "No. I'm serious," I say, "I can't remember the last time I went bowling and this could all go very badly."

I couldn't care less if I get a gutter or a strike, what I'm worried about is Nolan watching me walk, bend, and dip. I wouldn't want to watch my body do that.

"It'll be great," Nolan says, patting me on my back like we're in this together.

My cheeks puff with air that I slowly release. "Right. It'll be great."

The entire time I walk forward, all the things people

have said about me behind my back follow me, then I shake my head. Nolan would never do anything like that, would he? I release the ball. It lands in the gutter with a thud.

When I turn around, Nolan is trying not to laugh, and not doing a very good job of composing himself. "You weren't kidding," he says, still laughing.

I hold up a finger, attempting a *watch-this* gesture, but I have to wait for my ball to be spat back out of the machine so I can take my second turn. This time I manage to land the ball on the lane and take down a total of one pin.

Nolan slow-claps and then replicates my *watch-this* finger wave before he grabs his neon orange ball. He strides to the lane and right before he releases the ball he shakes his butt. All ten pins crash to the floor.

I'm desperately trying to keep the smile off my face. "Show-off."

"Are you referring to that"—he points to the lane behind him, then spins, and shakes his butt again—"or that?"

My cheeks flush. "Yes."

Nolan tries to look serious, but his smile betrays him. "It's the key to getting a strike. You should try," he says.

Before I can stop myself, I grab my ball, walk to the line, shake my butt at Nolan, and get another gutter ball. "Not exactly the key to a strike, is it?"

His arms encircle me. "Nope. But sure is cute."

Somewhere behind me, someone gets a strike and the explosion of pins ricochets through my chest. Maybe nobody got a strike, maybe that's just the sound of the walls around my heart shattering. This could be very dangerous.

Nolan grabs my ball, handing it to me before he puts his hands on my shoulders and steers me back toward the lane. He shows me the dots on the ground, then rests an arm on my shoulder, pointing to the arrows about halfway down. He says something about pretending I'm shaking hands with the pins and leaves me to my own devices. I manage to knock seven pins down, which is better than one. Or zero.

Nolan programs the computer to give me bumpers which improve my skill level, but he still beats me. By the time we start our third game, I remove the bumpers and do a decent job, even if I never manage to get a strike.

We return our shoes to the counter and Nolan takes my hand. "Want some pizza?" I nod and we find a table. There's a circular booth that could fit far more than just the two of us, but we take it and like Lady and the Tramp we meet in the middle. He bumps his shoulder against mine. "What are your feelings about pineapple on pizza?" he asks.

I flip my hair over my shoulder, wishing I had a hair tie to put it up. "It's not my favorite but it doesn't bother me. I draw the line at anchovies though." I almost dry heave.

Nolan's eyes are wide in shock. Either because I don't care if a pizza has pineapple or because it's not my favorite. There never seems to be a neutral opinion on Hawaiian pizza.

Then from across the room, someone shouts my name.

"Rindy!" Mina is waving a hand high above her head as she walks toward us.

If I was about to dry heave at the idea of little fish as pizza toppings, I'm really about to puke as Mina stops at our table. She gives Nolan a fist bump. "Hey, Nolan, haven't seen you much this summer. Your mom said Calvin's keeping you busy." Nolan nods but doesn't say anything about how working with his dad is going. Mina turns to me. "Thought you'd still be camping," she says.

Now it's my eyes that are about to pop out of my head. Of course, Nolan knows Mina. And of course, Nolan believes I'm staying at the B Hive, because that's where he found me. But housekeepers are never on a first-name basis with guests. Or know that their weekend plans included camping in the Redwoods with exceptionally cute boys.

"How do you know Rindy?" Nolan asks Mina.

Mina slides into the booth next to me. "She and I—"

"Mina helped me." I'm practically shouting. "I lost my necklace and when I realized, I went back to search the room —the room I share with my parents—and she was there. Cleaning. She helped me look. I guess I told her I was going camping." My eyes are as big as the pizza we have yet to order, and I blink several times, as the confused lines on Mina's forehead slowly smooth out.

Mina taps a fingernail on the table. "There you go. That's the story," she says.

A big fat lie of a story. I feel like a balloon deflating against the back of the booth. At any second Mina could tell

Nolan I'm lying, but she's choosing not to, and one day soon I'm going to have to explain all of this to her.

"No surprise Mina would be the one to find your necklace. Remember when you found Nibblets?" Nolan leans back, draping his arm around my shoulder. "Nibblets was a dog my parents used to have."

Mina scrapes at something on the table with her fingernail. "That dog could get out of a locked box." It makes Nolan laugh, and I'm once again reminded that there are a lifetime of details I'll never know. Mina pats the table. "Well, I'll leave you two alone. I need to go set up," she says as she scoots out of the booth.

The back of my head is on the red vinyl of the seat, and I take a deep breath. That was close, too close. When I tip my head forward again Nolan is busy with his phone. I wait until he's done, thankful that whatever he's doing has distracted him from Mina's appearance.

"Everything okay?" I ask.

Nolan pockets his phone. "A message from Lacie, she's doing better but feels horrible we had to leave because of her."

I jump on the chance to talk about anything other than Mina and the necklace I never lost. "You are such a good friend to Lacie."

"She's more than a friend." As soon as Nolan says it, all the color drains from his face.

The room starts spinning. This is it. This is the *I told you so* moment. What does Nolan mean by that? What does any of this mean? Our afternoon at the island. Camping. Today. Was it all a plot to get me to this moment so everyone could make fun of me? So everyone could have a good laugh at the plus-size girl on a date with the handsome local? Has it all been a pile of lies? I almost start laughing like a crazy person. I have no right to be concerned about lies, but this feels like the sharp blade of betrayal.

My words rush together. "You said you weren't dating. I asked and you said you weren't." I wish we were sitting at a table so I could get up and storm away because scooting along the bench until I can get out of this booth is not a very effective getaway.

My awkward scooting gives Nolan time to rush out his side of the booth and crash to his knees, blocking my exit. His face is still pale. "It's not like that. Let me explain."

His elbows are on the edge of the booth, and his hands cover his face. I want to run my hands through his hair or pull him close as one last reminder of what he felt like. I shouldn't want to do that. I should be halfway to the door by now.

Nolan rubs a hand at his neck and looks as if he's going to be sick. "You know how I told you that my dad bought the B Hive for my mom because he had an affair?" I don't understand where this is going but I nod. "And you know how Lacie doesn't know who her father is?" I pull all my hair over one shoulder, twisting it together in a haphazard attempt to calm down as I wait for Nolan to say something else.

He doesn't. And in the silence, every word he said turns

into grains of sand sifting through my mind until the solid rock of truth remains.

Nolan's dad had an affair.

Lacie doesn't know who her dad is.

Lacie is more than a friend to Nolan.

I slap a hand over my mouth. "Shut up. Lacie is your sister."

15

Nolan presses his hand to his lips. "Shh." He scans the restaurant over his shoulder like he's Jason Bourne clocking the exits. "Nobody knows. I was never supposed to find out." He weaves his fingers through mine, squeezing my hand but it might as well be a clamp around my heart when he says, "But I trust you."

Nolan trusts me. I want to slide out of the booth, or melt through the floor, so I don't have to stare into his pleading eyes that trust me. All I've done is lie, or tell him half-truths, which is the same thing. I do not deserve his trust.

The color returns to his face but he still doesn't look well. "You can't say anything. Promise me you won't tell anyone," he begs.

My answer is a silent nod and Nolan slides into the booth next to me again. This time I don't hesitate, I put my arms around him, pulling him close. I can't tell if it's his heart, or mine, that is pounding against my bones. There are a lot of secrets locked inside my heart, so adding one more doesn't seem like a big deal. But when I tuck this family secret next to everything else I don't want to share, it's heavier than I expect.

Nolan pulls back as his phone buzzes, tilting the screen so I can read a message from Lacie. She wants to know if she and Wick can join us.

The curious part of me wants to dig into this new revelation. How did Nolan find out Lacie was his sister? When did he find out? Is he ever going to tell her? Is this the reason he doesn't want to work for his father? Is he holding on to more secrets, the same way I am? Since Nolan almost passed out a moment ago, I don't think asking him more questions about discovering Lacie is his half-sister is a good idea. Plus, right now he's waiting for my answer, not more questions.

"Sure. Yes. Absolutely." Nolan raises his eyebrow, and I understand what he is silently asking—did he make a mistake in telling me this secret? I take a deep breath. "It's fine. I'm fine. I promise I won't say anything, and I promise it won't make things weird." I'm about to add that I'm an expert at keeping secrets, but that terrifies me because he might ask why.

He types a quick reply and almost instantly Lacie and Wick walk through the front door, straight to our table.

Nolan stands. "Were you—"

Lacie holds up a hand. "If you are about to ask if we were standing in the parking lot, yes, yes, we were. Be glad I texted. This moron"—she smacks her hand on Wick's chest—"was just going to walk in on your date."

Wick shakes his head as if he just woke up. "They're on a date?" But the light in his eyes says he already knew.

Nolan wraps Lacie in a hug and I watch her relax in his embrace. If I had seen this exchange ten seconds ago, jealousy would have swirled around my ankles, tripping me like an overgrown vine. And even though I know the truth, there's still a twinge that stabs just below my ribs. Not because I secretly wonder if Nolan loves Lacie, but because now I know he does. He's her family, she just doesn't know it.

I used to invent all kinds of family members for myself. Aunts and uncles. Strange but lovable cousins. But most of all, I invented siblings for myself, carloads of them. I named them and fought with them over stupid things in my mind. Like wasting all the hot water, hogging the remote, sitting on my cushion, or snooping in my room. We'd smack each other on the back of the head when no one was watching, and we'd beg to have our own rooms, but every night we'd say a silent prayer, thankful we were not alone.

I shove myself out of the booth. "Go ahead and order, I'll be right back." After the surprise visit from Mina, my lie, and then Nolan's revelation, I need a minute to myself.

The air freshener mounted to the bathroom wall is so strong I can taste it. It makes me want to push back through the door and go outside. But if I do that, Nolan will come and ask what I'm doing. And what I'm doing is trying not to pass out. Today has been a lot. Turning the sink handle to the left, I wait until steam wisps around the water then back it off and run my hands through it. The heat sends shivers down my spine, and I close my eyes at the simple pleasure of hot water. If only the beach access restroom had this modern-day marvel. I'm half tempted to somehow squish myself into the sink and pretend it's a bath, but I settle for washing my face.

Water drips from my chin as I wave my hand under the paper towel dispenser and someone exits from a stall behind me. I catch Mina's eye in the mirror and my heart plummets to my feet. We're locked in the reflective surface of the glass as Mina patiently washes her hands, never breaking eye contact with me. I've given up on ripping the paper towel off so I can dry my face. Mina finishes washing her hands and rips the dangling paper towel, handing it to me before getting some for herself.

She's standing in front of me, crumpling the paper towel into a ball, still not taking her eyes from me. I can't take her silence anymore. "I can explain," I say.

Mina raises her hand, stopping me from saying anything else. "Right now I need you to answer one question." She rubs two fingers across her bottom lip, and the weight of everything she might say presses against my chest. She stops rubbing her lip and asks, "Are you safe?"

It's the end of July but I feel like I slipped on a patch of black ice I didn't see in the dark. I know plenty of foster horror stories but none of them are my own. I never had a family, but I also never suffered abuse. Some of the girls I met at the group home were not as fortunate. They could never claim safety as their own.

This is not the question I was prepared for Mina to ask. She should have asked about the lies I've told. But she didn't. She asked if I was safe. I wish we were still standing side-by-side looking at each other in the mirror. It would somehow make this moment easier to handle.

I don't trust myself to say anything. I'm afraid that if I start to talk, everything I've kept hidden will slip out the cracked door of my lips, including Nolan's secret that I shoved on top of all the others. I nod, and when I do Mina's shoulders relax. "Okay then. Okay. That's all I need to know. For now." She tosses the wadded paper towel into the trash. "We'll talk tomorrow."

Mina pulls open the door, leaving me alone in the overly perfumed bathroom, clutching the paper towel she handed me. I finally wipe the water from my face and stare at my reflection. A mirage of Mina floats next to me in the mirror. *Are you safe?* I can hardly swallow past the lump at the back of my throat.

I am safe, but I'm also as close to the edge as I could possibly be. I'm a young homeless female, which is about as erasable of a demographic as there is. I have no family that would report me missing. I don't have a phone in case of an emergency. I have no idea how long it will take to scrape together enough cash to find a place to live because there are always more expenses than I plan for even when I'm painstakingly careful. I feel like all I have to do is sneeze and I'll fall off the cliff.

When Mina asked if I was safe, it was the closest I've been to being seen. My hands shake as I throw my paper towel away. Why was that her question? Does Mina understand that sometimes a person has to lie in order to survive?

As soon as I open the door, Wick's laughter rushes across the restaurant but my feet are stuck to the floor. Lacie, Wick, and Nolan. They have a gravitational pull, and I'm a hunk of space junk circulating their orbit.

The summer I turned twelve was magical. I was sent to a house where the living room had floor-to-ceiling windows that overlooked a forest and the mountains beyond. I had never seen anything more perfect. The family dressed like they were straight out of a photo shoot, and the moment I walked into that house, the mom wrapped me in a hug and told me I was going to have a great summer with them. And she was right, I did. They provided five weeks of respite foster care before I went back to a double-wide on a gravel road. It was perfect because they knew it had an expiration date. The clock started ticking the moment I arrived.

Clocks are always ticking. Nolan leaves at the end of the summer and whatever is brewing between us, time is going to run out. But right now, that's the least of my concerns. Mina said we would talk tomorrow, which means I might only have this afternoon left to pretend that the details of my life won't catch up with me.

Back at the table, Wick slides over to make room for me to sit. "Just in time," he says. "You have to cast the deciding vote between pineapple and the fruit haters."

Nolan looks at me, waiting for my vote, and I wish everything in life could be as simple as choosing pizza toppings.

Norma is not parked next to Hector in the supply room, and if this was a regular day I'd scan the halls for Mina to say good morning, but this is not a normal day. This is the day Mina said we needed to talk, and I don't feel like looking for her.

My daily room assignment is sitting on Hector's top shelf with a butterscotch candy resting on it like always. I pop the candy in my mouth, folding my schedule into my smock's front pocket. I'm not sure how long I can pretend today is a normal day. It all depends on how long it takes before Mina finds me. With every towel and stack of sheets that I pile on my cart, my arms get weaker, and my heart gets heavier. Mina knows I've flat-out lied to Nolan and I'm scared her knowledge of this could put everything else I'm trying to achieve for myself in jeopardy. Could I lose my job over this?

Will today be another *"one day this will all make sense"* moment of my life?

Pulling my hair into a ponytail, I push Hector to the elevator. There's nothing else for me to do except start my shift and hope I don't see Mina for a while.

The first room on my list is on the second floor. When the elevator doors slide open, and I back my cart out, I almost collapse to the ground. The room I've been assigned is 210 and Norma is parked in front of the adjacent room. Unless I can magically turn invisible, there is no way I can put off seeing Mina now. Did she plan this?

Last spring I helped Sylvia prune the apple trees that line the drive up to her house. In chopping off a branch I disturbed a bee nest. Only a few swarmed out, buzzing in a small cyclone between Sylvia and I before flying away. We were lucky they didn't descend upon us, but one landed on my finger and Sylvia climbed down her ladder, saying, "It'll either sting you or it won't."

It seemed like such a ridiculous thing for Sylvia to say. Of course those are the two options in that situation, getting stung or not, and that bee definitely stung me. I might as well be climbing the ladder in Sylvia's yard again as I carry my cleaning supplies into the bathroom. Talking with Mina will either sting or it won't.

I squirt cleaner into the toilet, then spray the counter and the tub before pulling all the towels into a pile. As I scrub, I keep expecting to hear Mina's voice behind me, but besides the pounding of my heart, the room is silent as I work. It's not until after I've finished cleaning the bathroom and stripped the bed that Mina enters the room.

I'm holding the giant snowball of sheets when she asks, "What's the worst part of housekeeping?"

Instead of depositing the bundle of sheets onto my cart in the hall, I drop them at my feet. "The beds."

"Exactly." Mina walks toward the king-size one I'm about to remake. "People always assume the toilets are the worst part, but I guarantee hotel toilets have a better flush-to-brush ratio than their throne at home."

I snort, because she's not wrong. And I'm glad for this little moment of normality as I try to forget she might be a bee landing on my finger. "I'm just glad there are no bunk beds here. Those are the worst," I say.

"Yep, do enough of those and you've done your cardio for the day."

I return from Hector with a fresh stack of sheets, thankful for something to hold. If I didn't have the sheets, I'd be fiddling with my hair, braiding it and unbraiding it, waiting for whatever Mina is going to say next. As I send the fitted sheet flying over the mattress like a sail Mina starts talking.

"I've been trying to figure out what I should say." She shakes her head as if all her words are clumped together and she's trying to knock one loose. Instead, she just grabs the corner of the sheet, pulling it over the mattress. "I wasn't much older than you are when I walked through the door of a women's shelter." At that, I let go of the sheet. Mina is not looking at me, and she just keeps making the bed. "My parents weren't exactly around, and I was dating a nasty piece of work. It took me longer than it should have before I was brave enough to leave him."

Mina's finished her half of the bed now and she walks to my side where I haven't done a single thing to make the bed. "You told me you're safe, so I'll take your word for it. I'm not going to demand you tell me why you're lying because if I was in your shoes, I wouldn't have told the truth at the time either." Mina finishes putting the fitted sheet on the bed as I stand there, too shocked to help or speak. "Walking into that shelter was the scariest thing I ever did. It was scarier than covering over bruises with lies and foundation because I was finally admitting the truth." She takes a breath. "But it changed my life. Beverly was just out of college, and she ran that shelter. She helped me get my first job. And then, when she got this place up and running, I was the first person she hired."

My mouth hangs open. There is a lot to digest, but I cannot get past one detail. "Beverly ran a women's shelter?" Mina nods and I back up several steps, circling the room we are standing in with its black and white and gold décor, like the rest of this boutique inn. "Beverly Lambert used to run a shelter for women?"

It's Mina's turn to give a soft snort. "The one and only. A lot can happen to change a person, but she still has the same heart." She takes a breath and slowly lets it out. "Even if it's underneath a lot more pressure and polish these days."

I pick up a pillow, hugging it to my chest. I don't know what to do or what to say. Mina isn't the kind of person to take crap from anyone, but she's just admitted that she did. She used to be abused, and lived in a shelter until she found her way. A shelter that Beverly ran.

I struggle to wrap my head around it all as she tosses me a case for the pillow I'm strangling and says, "I might not know what's going on in your life, but if you ever want to trust me, I'm here and not going anywhere."

Mina waits as I stuff the pillow into the case. I can barely make my hands work, let alone my mouth. Everyone who has ever known me has always let me down. Even Sylvia, who meant so much to me.

I asked her once if I could live with her. When I did, the kindness in her eyes was covered over by sadness and I spoke again before she could tell me no. I understood, she could only offer me so much and I gladly took what she could give, even if I wanted more. She was the only one who knew I was leaving, not because I told her, but because she had a sense about those kinds of things, like knowing it was going to snow without looking at the sky.

The night before I left, we sat on her porch and she said, "People get all excited at the start of a hike, and they're happy when it's over because they accomplished something." She had looked at me. "But the only thing that gets a person from the beginning to the end, is their willingness to keep going."

Mina watches me struggle to get the pillow into the

fabric, but I do, and I toss it on the bed. When it's clear I'm not going to say anything, she says, "I mean it, Rindy. If you're ever ready. I'm right here."

She walks out of the room and seconds later Norma glides past the open door. I crumple on the end of the bed, my body tipping forward, head in my hands. I am so tired of trying to hold myself together. I'm tired of lying. I'm tired of sleeping on the ground. I'm tired of having to be grateful for every handout that has ever been tossed vaguely in my direction.

But more than being tired, I want to make it on my own. I don't want to owe anybody any sort of *thank you, ma'am* or explanation of my life. If I can manage to hang on for a few more months no one will care that I never had a family and aged out of the system. No one cares about preschool achievements when you reach high school, and no one cares about high school achievements when you are climbing corporate ladders. I need to make it out of this hole before I tell anyone I've been trapped in it.

I stand up too fast and the room spins, and it's not the only thing spinning. Everything Mina said swirls in my head. *If you ever want to trust me.* But that's the thing, I don't know how. I can want something and never have it. That's the story of my life.

I don't remember finishing the room. Or the next. Or any of the rooms on my list. The only thing I could hold in my head was Mina saying *if you ever want to trust me* and I spent the rest of the day playing a mental game of tug-of-war.

I'm so drained that by the end of my shift, I walk straight to the entrance at the front of the lobby. I'm almost out the door when I remember I'm still wearing my smock. Walking back to the supply room, I can't even remember if I put Hector away, but sure enough, he's parked next to Norma where he belongs. Opening my locker, I see the pile of clothes I pulled from my backpack and remember I was going to do laundry this afternoon. Shoving everything in my backpack, I head to the bathroom and change into the one dress I own.

This time when I exit through the main doors of the B Hive, I run smack into someone's chest. "I'm so sorry," I say, but my apology is muffled against this person's T-shirt. I'm already off-balance and it confuses me even more when this person hugs me until I smell a familiar body spray and something else that reminds me of the wind.

Nolan's voice is so close to my ear. "I was on my way to find you," he says.

It should be a thrill that the boy I like more than I'll admit was looking for me, but it's one more thing to add to the events that have rattled me today. Mina lived in a shelter. Beverly ran the shelter. Mina wants me to trust her. Nolan almost saw me walk out of the B Hive wearing a house-keeping apron.

"I didn't want you to think I forgot about the deal we made," he says.

I have no idea what deal we made because my brain malfunctioned hours ago. My face scrunches as I try to recol-lect details, but all I can pull to the surface are bee stings and

Mina's words. For the first time, I wonder if I shouldn't have thought that about Mina, that she'll either sting me or not. What if there was a third option I never considered? An option where she understood?

"You don't remember?" Nolan asks and I'm silent while he reminds me with an arched eyebrow. "You come camping with me and I said I'd teach you how to swim. I was thinking we could go up to the house and have your first lesson."

My mind is full of Mina and bees and beds under canoes and shelters. Now is not the time to learn how to swim. I need to go do my laundry and then walk to the ocean and stare at the crashing waves while I try to understand how people decide to trust someone with the truth. I do not need swimming lessons.

But Nolan is here with his hands on my shoulders, and it feels like a lifeline, so I say, "Perfect. Let's go."

17

We don't talk much on the walk, which is fine with me. I'm not sure what I'd manage to say if Nolan started a conversation; my brain is still mush. I can't shake the image of Beverly running a women's shelter out of my mind. It does not match the person I've come to know. Beverly is streamlined and sleek, she wants everything to be homogeneous. And I'm guessing a shelter would be the opposite of that word. Mina says Beverly is still the same person, but it's hard for me to believe. Yet looks can be deceiving, I know that for a fact.

Nolan's house is a replica of the B Hive from the outside. Black shutters stand out against the white paint, and I wonder if the interior is decorated with gold accents. I can't believe Nolan grew up in a mansion on a hill overlooking the rugged Pacific Ocean. Our lives could not be more opposite.

Maybe he can read my mind because as we walk up the driveway, he glances over his shoulder with a strange look in his eye, almost like an apology, rubbing a hand across his chin. He hasn't shaved since we went camping. Is it because yesterday as we ate our pineapple-free pizza I told him he should keep the woodsman look? Why would he care what I think?

We curve around the garage following a path of square pavers with grass sprouting in neat lines between them. I am more relaxed in the backyard surrounded by ancient pines. With my back to the house, it's easy to forget I don't belong anywhere near a place like this.

The pool glitters up at me and I remember why we've come here. Swimming lessons are a horrible idea. I need to do laundry. It's not the only thing I need to do. I need to tell Nolan the truth, but admitting everything I've kept hidden feels awkward now. I seriously need to think of something to say that can get me out of this swim lesson, but my brain is still malfunctioning.

"You can change in there." Nolan points to a small building near the pool and I veer off in that direction. I don't need to change because I do not own a swimsuit. But he's expecting me to and I'm curious what lies behind the door. It'll also buy me a moment to myself and maybe I can figure out what to do.

The floor is nonslip tile and there's a sauna behind a separate door, a toilet behind another door, a rack of soft, plush towels, and a bench. I almost cry at the sight of the shower. A massive rainhead descends from the ceiling, and four nozzles poised at different angles protrude from the walls. It reminds me of a carwash. It would be heaven to turn it on. Forget swimming, I want to spend the rest of the day taking a shower.

Nolan shouts from outside. "Could you bring me a towel when you come out?"

"Sure," I shout back. This isn't exactly a pool house, it's more like a five-star bathroom, and I could live here. It's a much better situation than rolling under a canoe every night and sponging myself off with ice-cold water in a public restroom.

I wonder what Beverly thinks of this bathroom. Does she think it's beneath her to use since it's basically a shed in her backyard? I catch my reflection in the mirror and take a deep breath. I hate when people hear the words *foster kid* and already have their minds made up about who I am. Or who I'm not. It takes a certain kind of person to care enough about other people to run a women's shelter. I should stop assuming Beverly is judging the entire world by impossibly high standards, even if I think it's true.

Water splashes against the side of the pool as I blow out a puff of air. Nolan is waiting for me, and I need to figure out what I'm going to do about my first-ever swimming lesson. I have on the only dress I own, which is more of a muumuu than an actual dress. Underneath I'm wearing a sports bra and bike shorts. I found all of this at a garage sale, and for seventy-five cents this has become my Oh Suds Up outfit so I can wash everything I own at once.

Swimming is not a life skill I need, I've made it this far

and survived. I don't want to explain to Nolan why I agreed to this when I don't even own a swimsuit. I want to close my eyes and disappear. Actually, what I'd really like is to own a swimsuit like a normal person.

If my brain was working it would be screaming at me right now, shouting at me to stop. But my arms lift my dress over my head and fold it on the bench. Maybe it's better this way. Nolan will see me for what I am—disgusting—and run the other way. It's happened before. I might as well break whatever spell he thinks I've cast because I'm the only person he knows who wants to go to the Pando.

Nolan floats like a starfish before sinking under the water and swimming to the other side of the pool, with only a few bubbles breaking the surface. His head pops up and he wipes the water from his eyes. He spots me standing next to a lounge chair and glides in my direction like a strange sea otter with only his head above the surface.

"You didn't buy that green bikini?" he asks, crossing his arms on the pool deck. His smile flashes like a hazard sign.

Oh great, he remembers the green bikini. My stomach drops anchor to my feet. "That would never fit—" I twist my hands into a knot. "In my budget." I'm nervous and can't believe I said that. "Plus. Why would I need a bikini when I don't know how to swim? Pointless. So. This is what you get." Untying the knot of my hands, I wave them in front of my body, showcasing the lime-green sports bra and hot pink bike shorts. What is wrong with me? *This is what you get.* I never want to speak again.

Nolan heaves himself out of the pool and I'm confident I've proved my point, he doesn't want to be anywhere near me. But he drips a trail of water until he stands in front of me. "This is what I love about you. You are completely unafraid to be yourself."

What is he talking about? Being myself has never gone well, and I have a long list of receipts to prove that. This was supposed to be another point on the list, the moment when I reveal something about myself, about my body, and he covers his eyes. But Nolan is standing in front of me dripping water at our feet, smiling his stupidly adorable smile.

I'm so confused by him that for once my fear of being seen is shoved out of the way by my desire to belong and I admit something true. "I'm terrified."

His forehead scrunches and he rests a hand on my shoulder. "Of what?"

His high-voltage smile and beautiful eyes for starters. The truth. Feeling like a towering mound of soft-serve sherbet and the fact that my heart is tapping against my ribs in a way it never has before. I'm afraid that I'm too much, and not enough, all at the same time. But revealing one truth is more than enough for my inexperienced heart.

"Drowning." It's all I say.

Nolan's smile is the north star. "Do you trust me?"

I almost collapse onto the lounge chair. Twice in one day? Mina wants me to trust her. Nolan is asking me if I already do. Before today, if I had to write a list of trustworthy people in my life, I'd start with Sylvia and not know what to do after that. I suddenly ache to spill my guts to Mina and watch her clean them up. I want her to mop my life story up off the floor, wring it out, and dump away everything ugly. But my desire to trust Mina is overshadowed by all my fears.

Nolan on the other hand is a completely different story.

Trusting him is easy because my heart is too far ahead of my mind. I nod and he grabs my hand, leading me toward the stairs at the opposite end of the pool. As we descend he says, "In senior year I was nominated for the school's outstanding sportsmanship award. I played shortstop all four years. It's not like scouts came looking, but I was good enough to keep playing if I wanted to. I just didn't want to." Our feet touch the bottom of the pool as cool water sloshes against our abdomens. "Anyway. There was this big assembly and right as I walked on stage, Wick rushed up and pantsed me. He got everything and let me tell you, that stage got really breezy, really fast."

This story is such an unexpected diversion from everything I'm feeling that I laugh so hard I have to wipe a tear from my cheek. "Why are you telling me this?"

Nolan tips back so he's floating, scuttling water back and forth with his hands, spinning a slow circle around me. "Because none of this is some sort of joke to me. I'd never let anything bad happen to you."

I can't let myself cry right now, but my eyes sting so I cover my face with my hands. All I've ever been is an added responsibility to foster families and the great state of Montana. The system worked as well as a broken system can work, which means it hardly worked at all. I haven't known Nolan for very long and yet no one has ever made me feel as safe as he does. It's a relief, but it's also a burden I don't know how to carry.

"Whoa, hey, what's wrong?" He stands next to me and when I uncover my face, I see the worry on his.

"No one has ever—" I swallow, unsure what to tell him, and end up pushing a mouthful of air out my mouth that makes my lips flap. "I've never done this. Relationships—of any kind—never work. Never." Pulling all my hair to one side I twist it into a knot and let my hands fall into the water with a splash. "I don't understand why you say things like this to me. No one ever likes me."

Nolan steps closer. Then closer. "Do you trust me?" They are the same words he said a moment ago, but this time a different flame heats the question.

"Yes." It's barely a whisper.

Nolan's eyes are a more radiant blue than the water we are standing in. "I don't know who hurt you, but that's something I'll never do. I will never hurt you," he says.

His words hold the comfort of a knife because it's everything I've wanted, and nothing I ever allowed myself to believe would happen. The worst part is that I believe him right now. Nolan is not just saying this, I can't imagine him ever hurting anyone.

His hand slides from the side of my face to the back of my head as he pulls me toward him. I want to trust Nolan with everything, but I'm not sure I can unzip my heart and show him my story. It's agonizingly slow before his lips touch mine, soft and gentle, an invitation I accept, and when I do, a million fireworks are set off from the dock of my heart.

Every doubt disappears in a rush. All that is left is the gentle splash of water against the side of the pool, and the rustle of branches high above our locked-together bodies. I never knew kissing was like eating cotton candy—sweet, gone too fast, and instantly leaving me hungry for more.

<h1 style="text-align:center">18</h1>

Learning to swim felt a lot like drowning, but Nolan said I was catching on quickly. I could have done without the lesson, but the kissing and then a scorching hot shower were both worth it. I didn't expect Nolan to hand me a motorcycle helmet as soon as I emerged from the luxury bathroom.

A drip of water slides down my spine from my braid, leaving a shiver in its wake. "What's this for?" I ask.

Nolan shushes me with a click of his tongue and a raised eyebrow as he grabs my hand, leading me around the front to the open garage. A vintage Harley sits next to a parked Lexus.

Nolan's smile is a fire starter, and I try asking again. "What's going on?"

But all I get is another playful smile and I have to restrain myself from covering his lips with mine. I'm in so much trouble. He's leaving. I'm staying. I can't get carried away. Nolan kicks the engine to life and the roar of it reverberates through my bones. Where are we going? How am I supposed to stay on this thing? Where do I put my hands? What happens when we go around a corner? I push all the questions away and swing my leg over the seat.

The road rushes under my feet. I have never wished I was a bird until this moment. This is what freedom feels like.

At Gov's house, for a few months I shared a room with a girl who always had dreams she was flying. She'd wake up and tell me what it felt like to pass through the center of a cloud. At the time I was jealous, because my dreams were populated with locked doors, broken glass that cut the bottoms of my feet, and empty cardboard boxes. I wish I knew where that girl ended up because now, I could tell her I understand, and the best part is, this isn't a dream.

Half an hour later Nolan pulls to a stop in a patch of dirt on the side of the highway. As we stow our helmets I say, "I didn't know you had a motorcycle."

His smile fades as he pats the seat. "My dad would kill me if he knew I took it." Nolan attempts a dangerous smile, but it looks cautious. "He leaves it in the garage, tempting me with the keys dangling from the ignition, so it's basically his fault. Besides, he's gone until next week."

We step over knotted pine roots that make a ladder on the ground before hiking through the forest. After a time, the trees give way to cliffs, and we might as well be on another planet. A massive rock forms a natural bridge, with the ocean raging below, and in the distance, several small rocky islands jut from the sea. We keep walking until the ground narrows to a point barely big enough for the two of us. Nolan sits, his legs dangling off the side of the earth as he motions to the ground next to him, and I lower myself down.

I can't believe what's in front of my eyes. It's one of the most incredible views I've ever seen. A sheer cliff for more miles than I can imagine is to our right, the ocean is in front of us, beneath us, surrounding us. I wish I could stay right here, in this thin line where the sky kisses the earth. Heat rises up my back at the memory of kissing Nolan and I steal a glance at him. Does he regret what happened earlier? The wind whips his hair across his face and he's looking right at me.

This time his smile spreads all the way to his eyes. "I knew you'd like it here."

I brush the hair off his face. "Won't you be sad to leave all this?"

He grabs my hand, his hair blowing every which way again, and kisses my palm, then weaves our hands together as if he's making a fence to protect what he just gave me. My internal temperature rises several degrees. "Do you ever wonder about all the lives you could have lived?" he asks.

He's kidding, right? That is exactly what my life has been, all day every day, picturing all the lives I could have had. Parents. Siblings. Stepparents. Grandparents. I've never cared what tree I climbed as long as it was a family tree. What would make Nolan wonder about other lives? Does he wonder what it would be like to agree to his dad's plan for his life? Is it more than that?

"I used to," I admit.

After a long stretch of silence, Nolan squeezes my hand. "What will you do when you get home?"

I'm lost inside the majestic landscape that is ever-shifting in front of me. Not to mention the sensation of holding hands with Nolan, his kiss trapped between our palms. "Laundry."

His laugh rivals the crash of waves breaking on the rock below us. "Okay, sure, but are you going to college in the fall? Work?" A silent *or something else* takes shape at the end of his question.

I can't believe my first thought of home was the canoe rack. But that's not what he is asking. Nolan wants to know what I'm going to do when I go home to Montana, a place I have no intention of returning to because I don't have a family to go home to.

"I'm not going back." But the wind took my words and Nolan leans closer, making me repeat myself. It's the first time I've voiced my plans, and it feels nice to have said them. I've finally offered Nolan a shred of truth.

I don't know what I'll do if he asks me why I don't want to go back, but he doesn't, he just says, "Rindy the Wayfarer." Like it's the title of a book he wants to read.

It makes me sound adventurous, but I'm not. I'm Rindy the Homeless. Rindy the Abandoned. Rindy the Desperate.

"If you could go anywhere in the world right now, would it still be to the Pando?" Nolan asks, his eyes searching mine.

"Yes, but dreams are costly." It's going to take months before I can scrape together enough money to find a place to live. I can't afford to have dreams right now, not when having a place to sleep that isn't tucked under a rotting canoe is out of reach.

Nolan sits up a little straighter. "Costly. Like staying the entire summer at the B Hive?" He squints at me. "Your parents must be nothing like you. I can imagine you out here in the wild open places. Not shut inside the Hive all summer."

I've never met my parents. I can't understand what would drive someone to abandon their infant daughter at a gas station, and I've never once felt like defending either of them until this moment. Except it's not those parents I'm defending. It's the ones I created that love me and took me on a summer-long vacation to California.

"Maybe you don't know me as well as you think you do," I say, trying to make it sound flirty but it just sounds like the truth. I nudge Nolan with my shoulder and laugh. I don't want to argue with him, I want everything to feel like it did when we were in the pool, but I've ruined that. So, I tell him something else that's true. "Maybe you know me better than anyone."

But maybe it's too late.

19

Smelling like dryer sheets is better than smelling like whatever funk my backpack has become. I should have done laundry yesterday, but the gift of a panoramic ocean view, and kissing Nolan was worth the delay, even if I'm still not sure what he's thinking. I should be okay with the fact that I probably ruined my chances with Nolan; it's bound to happen sooner or later, so why not now? Why not accept the gift of spending time with him for what it was and move on? It's what I should do, along with my laundry, instead of walking to Lacie's house.

There was no answer when I knocked on Lacie's front door, so I decide to try her grandmother's market on Lambert Avenue. Half a block from the market on a side street, Lacie's head pokes out an open door, her smile bigger than she is.

"I was looking for you," we say at the same time and both start laughing.

"You were looking for me inside—" I step closer to see what store she is hanging out of.

"Oh, this is my mom's place." She waves me into the yoga studio. The front is all glass, and one wall is entirely made up of mirrors which make the room appear larger than it is. Two women emerge from a room at the back. "Mom. Poh Poh. This is my friend Rindy, the one I told you about."

Lacie's mom gives me a hug. "I'm Jade. Thanks for taking care of my baby girl on the camping trip. We heard it was quite the experience." Her eyes lock on Lacie's and I wonder how many stories Lacie told from the trip.

I start to stammer an explanation that I didn't do much of anything to take care of Lacie, that was mostly Nolan, but I only get a few words out before Lacie's grandmother taps her walking stick against Lacie's leg.

"Good, two bodies now." Poh Poh walks past Lacie toward the front window. "Sloths move faster. Come." Her walking stick thumps the ground.

Lacie rolls her eyes, but they are smiling. "Don't mind her, her love language is short little sentences."

"And occasional smacks from her cane?" I ask.

Lacie follows her grandmother, tugging me along. "Oh yes, it's how you know you're loved."

Poh Poh is on the sidewalk, standing on a tipped-over crate in front of the widow looking into the studio. I'm not sure she should be perching on that wobbly box. "I don't have all day," shouts Poh Poh. Then again, she seems surprisingly feisty.

"Mom, did you even ask them?" Jade stands between Lacie and me, her hands on our shoulders, giving them a squeeze. "You don't have to do this if you don't want to," she tells us.

Lacie's mom is shorter than Lacie but they have the same slender body and jet-black hair except Jade's is missing the electric blue tips. "Do what?" I ask.

Lacie answers. "Mom wants Poh Poh to trace the outlines of a bunch of people on the window with the slogan *Yoga is for EveryBODY*. Cheesy, right." Lacie makes a face, then turns to her mom, giving her a hug. "But also really cool," Lacie says.

There are so many better options than being traced onto a piece of glass, pretty much anything would be better than that. But on my first day in Tinlee Bay, I was practically chased out of a store by the lady with pouty lips. I don't like people looking at my body because it usually ends with a joke. Then I remember my first swimming lesson. Nolan has seen plenty of me and he has never said anything rude. At least not yet. If Jade wants to make sure everyone feels welcome in her studio no matter their size, that's something I'd like to be a part of. Even if it means having an imprint of myself stamped on the window.

I swallow all my lingering doubt and say, "Sounds good."

Lacie makes me ditch my backpack in the corner and then poses my arms several times before she is satisfied with one down and one on my hip. Then she stands next to me, mirroring my position. We stare out the window while Poh Poh begins tracing my form with a black paint marker.

"You were looking for me?" Lacie asks.

I nod, but when Poh Poh shoots her eyes into mine I decide to hold very still. "I have a favor to ask." I'm thankful that I'm not facing Lacie for this next part and rush ahead. "Nolan invited me to his mom's fundraiser, and I don't have anything to wear."

Lacie is no longer posing, which is okay I guess since Poh Poh is only working on tracing my body onto the window, but she grabs my arm, which is not okay because Poh Poh shouts something I can't understand, and Lacie drops it again.

"Wait. Back up. Nolan is going to his mom's gala, and he invited you?" Lacie asks.

A gala sounds worse than a fundraiser. What did I agree to? I want to turn my head to read Lacie's expression, but I don't dare. Turns out I don't have to because Lacie wedges herself between me and the window as another volley of angry-sounding words erupts from Poh Poh. Lacie shouts back her own and then squints at me. I swear she's about to lean forward and sniff me, a bloodhound on the trail of a juicy story.

My face reddens under her inspection and all my nervous doubts are laid bare beneath Lacie's magnifying glass. I'm suddenly annoyed. Is she upset because Nolan asked me and not her? "Is that such a bad thing?" I ask.

"No. Not bad, just unusual." Poh Poh's walking stick thuds against the window and Lacie scoots next to me, hand on her hip, her face a warped reflection next to mine.

Maybe Lacie doesn't believe every*body* is welcome in Nolan's life. My skin bristles and I want to push this conversation until we're arguing. It's a sensation I haven't had since living at Gov's house. That place was a petri dish, growing new arguments and resentment daily. Wanting to start an argument with Lacie right now feels like pulling a safety blanket across my back.

My shoulders are firm. "Unusual that Nolan would want to ask someone like me?"

"What does that even mean, '*someone like you*'?" Lacie waits half a second before continuing. "It's unusual because one, Nolan is actually going and two, he's taking a date."

Even in the reflection, I catch a hidden expression in Lacie's eyes before she smiles. "I'm not blind," she says. "I see the way he looks at you. I've known Nolan my whole life and I've never seen him act like this with anyone." She holds up her hands, palms out. "Not gonna lie, I used to want him to look at me like that. I wanted to be his person, you know. But he made it very clear that was never going to happen. Ever. Which was maybe the most embarrassing moment of my life, but somehow, he stuck around."

Nolan's family secret is a flare burning in my chest. I know who Lacie's father is. I know why Nolan stuck around to be Lacie's friend. Because she's his sister, and even if Nolan can't tell Lacie the truth, he'd never leave her alone.

Truth is a funny beast. We always want it but it's hard to give. At least it's hard for me to hand out, because my truth always seems like a bunch of goat's heads stuck to me after hiking through the brush. They hurt and are hard to get rid of. As much as I dislike lying, at least it's not as painful as pulling the truth off my skin. Poh Poh's eyes flash to mine as she finishes tracing my face, moving her marker to outline my torso. I'm not the only one not telling the truth. Nolan has never told Lacie he's her half-brother. Is he afraid to tell her? Maybe keeping important details under lock and key is another way Nolan and I are similar.

Lacie keeps talking. "Not that Nolan ever lacks female attention, because, well, you've seen him." She laughs. "He just never returns the attention, you know what I mean?" She shrugs, puffing her cheeks out. "Anyway. Gala. Date. No outfit." All of a sudden she squeals. "Does this mean you need to go on a shopping spree?" The last two words float up in hopeful expectation.

My lips pinch together. "Yes. Well, not exactly. I have zero money so I was hoping we could find something at a thrift shop." I wince at the idea. How could I ever find something appropriate for a gala Beverly is throwing at a second-hand shop? I might need to breathe into a paper bag. I keep conveniently forgetting Beverly is going to be at this event, and how am I supposed to avoid her when I'll be there with Nolan? I shouldn't spend any of my zero dollars on an outfit I'll wear once.

This is a horrible idea, but before I can take back anything I said, Lacie chef kisses her fingers.

"Are you kidding! Repurposing clothes is my thing." Lacie shouts over her shoulder. "Mom, we're going to need a ride!"

20

Jade drives us to Eureka, dropping us at a store called Do-Over. I wring my hands as we enter, hoping this afternoon won't end up on the list of things I want to take back and do over in my life. As we walk in, we practically run into the headless mannequin with marker tattoos scribbled up and down its arms, displaying a very small, very tight silver sequin dress. I'm not the sort of person who finds hidden treasures in a store like this. Stores like this have small dresses in equally small sizes. What was I thinking? I should save my money and Nolan and myself all the trouble by telling him I can't go.

Lacie is practically glowing as she scans the rows of racks. She stretches her arms before popping her knuckles, then looks me over from head to toe as she says, "Time to work my magic."

Lacie has lightning hands, pulling hangers off the rack

and putting them back all in the blink of an eye. I don't know what her decision-making process is, but so far, every item has been rejected. Eventually, she hands things my way and clothes start to drip off both my arms. There is not an employee in the dressing area to ask how many items we have, which is good because when I dump everything to the ground it's a haystack of clothes. Crop tops and skirts of all styles, ruched dresses, a pair of tuxedo slacks, an old wedding dress, and I'm not even sure what else.

Lacie kisses three fingers like I'm Katniss headed into the arena. "Good luck in the room of doom," she says.

"The room of doom?" I echo.

She pats her palm against the dressing room door. "These are torture chambers. So, good luck."

I cock my head to the side. What could Lacie have against trying clothes on? Everything looks good on her. "You hate dressing rooms?"

"Doesn't everybody? I was almost strangled by a sports bra once. My mom had to crawl under the door and save me." She hugs herself. "Plus, the lighting is always horrific and reminds you why you hate mirrors in the first place. Everything always looks better on the hanger than it does on your body." She shrugs. "So, yeah, not my favorite."

She hands me the first thing off the top of the pile. It's a pale pink dress with a zipper down the front and I can't imagine how this would be appropriate for a gala that Beverly is throwing. I raise one eyebrow.

"You never know." Lacie shrugs. "Fashion gods are fickle."

It doesn't matter if this is gala-approved or not, because I can't get the dress past my hips and fling it over the top of the door, trying not to catch sight of every square inch of my skin in the mirror as I wait for whatever comes next. How can Lacie not like what she sees in the mirror? Another dress lands on my head. It's a deep forest green, and when I put it on it's baggy in all the wrong places. I open the door, expecting Lacie to laugh. She doesn't.

Lacie pinches her bottom lip between her fingers and says, "Within the realm of possibility."

After that, I lose track of what I try on, but by the end of our tennis match of outfits flung back and forth over the door, Lacie has sorted the initial pile into two. The pile containing clothes that could work is pathetically small. Lacie isn't bothered by that because she grabs two and marches to the register with a confidence I'll never have in a clothing store. All I can see is the mass of wrinkled green fabric dragging behind Lacie along with the old wedding dress. As thankful as I am to be out of the room of doom, those cannot be the top choices.

Both dresses are a total of five dollars, and normally that would have me mentally congratulating myself for finding such great deals, but I feel like a dog backed into a corner guarding my wallet, hackles raised. Is it because I'm not sure what Lacie is going to do with these purchases? Why am I even going through with this? I can't walk into a room wearing an old wedding dress with beads and tulle and hope Beverly won't notice me.

"I can't do this." I push the dresses and they almost fall off the counter. "This is a really bad idea."

Lacie braces her hands on my shoulders. "I'm Edna Mode, okay, so trust me."

I can't understand her because my heart is pounding in my ears. "Edna who?"

"The Incredibles. Edna makes their costumes." My face remains blank. "Never mind. I know what I'm doing. Trust me."

Mina. Nolan. Lacie. They all want me to trust them, and they throw the word around like it's a standard-issue human response. As if I should want to trust people because they'll take care of me. I don't trust anyone, but I still pull a crumpled five-dollar bill out of my pocket. My breath catches at the back of my throat. "Fine."

Lacie grabs the two dresses off the counter with a triumphant smile. I have no idea how this is going to be anything but a disaster. I don't want to walk into the gala looking like a shriveled garden pea or the bride of Frankenstein, but I guess trust is putting my fate in someone else's hands. I hope I don't regret this.

21

It's been a week since Mina asked me if I could trust her, and I miss chatting with her in the supply room or as we pass in the hall. It's not like she's the one ignoring me. She tries starting a conversation every time I see her. I'm the one ignoring her, sometimes choosing to communicate with mute blinks, hoping she'll be able to translate them, but I probably look like I have something in my eye.

Today, Mina and I are tasked with transforming the dining room into a gala-approved hall, which means four hours of overtime on my next paycheck, so I'm not complaining, even if it was harder than normal to ignore Mina. I kept myself busy in the corners away from her, not only because I don't want to talk to her, but because I'm mentally coming up with strategies of how I'll be able to avoid Beverly in a few hours.

When Mina and I are finally done she says, "You seemed kind of stressed this afternoon."

I'm more surprised than her when I answer. "I have to go pick up my dress for the gala tonight, but it's going to be a disaster."

Mina's face brightens as she steps closer. She reaches out her hand like she's about to put it on my shoulder but changes her mind, grabbing her necklace, and twisting a finger through the chain. "Oh, I have made myself a tribe out of my true affections." The words are a riddle I don't understand and my face scrunches. "It's a line from my favorite Stanley Kunitz poem," she offers as an explanation.

I offer another mute blink. I should do three short blinks followed by three long ones because I am in serious trouble and maybe Mina would recognize SOS. But I just stare at her silently and when she leaves a moment later, I grip the edge of Hector for support. Who is Mina? She looks at me with more understanding than I'm willing to admit and recites lines of poetry that feel like echoes of my own heartbeat.

Could I make my own tribe? Is that even possible? Is this what is happening with Nolan, Wick, and Lacie? It's something I'll have to think about later because unless I want to wear my worn-out leggings to the gala, I need to get my dress. I'm not sure I'll survive the gala, and I'm not convinced I'll even have the guts to go, but I need to see what Lacie created.

After we got back from Do-Over, Lacie measured me and said I couldn't see the final product until she finished. I don't know what awaits me, but I hope it's not the disaster I've been envisioning. Rushing up to the studio, I see more traced outlines grace the window. They are all so different and it's not only the poses, but also the bodies themselves. I love how they fit together. For the first time I trace my finger along the drawn curve of my waist. Maybe I don't see myself the same way other people do, because my outline is nice. Life really would be boring if we all looked the same.

Almost all the lights are off inside, and I pull the door open with a tentative hello. Poh Poh appears in the doorway of the backroom. "Lacie's not here. Already at work. Come." I didn't know Lacie was working but can't help smiling as I remember this is Poh Poh's love language. What is she like when she gets mad? I hope I never find out.

The rubber soles of Poh Poh's sneakers squeak across the hardwood as she walks to a different doorway in the back. I follow her in and hanging on an open door of a small square locker is the most beautiful dress I've ever seen.

"Oh." The word slips out as I press my fingers to my mouth.

Poh Poh's cane taps twice on the ground. "Yes. Lacie is very talented."

The lace halter bodice of the wedding dress had been a stained, dingy gray, but somehow Lacie transformed it into a luscious cream, and attached it to the skirt of the green ball-gown that bunched in all the wrong places. Together they are a seamless masterpiece.

"I'll wait. You'll need help with the zipper," Poh Poh says

as she sits on a wooden bench and I take the dress into the bathroom.

Holding my breath I slide the fabric on, afraid I'll ruin its beauty. Once it's over my head, it becomes my second skin, as if I'm the only person who can bring the dress to life. I woke up early this morning so I'd have time to wash my hair in the glacial sink water—which gave me an instant headache —but I knew that having clean hair would be worth it. I'd even sectioned my hair into four braids, which looked ridiculous, so I hid them under a bandana all day. But now, pulling the fabric off my head to undo the braids, I rake my fingers through soft waves.

It's Poh Poh's turn to let out a quiet *oh* as she stands. She zips me in before practically pushing me into the studio toward the wall of mirrors. She's behind me now so it's hard to tell, but she smiles. I don't believe the reflection belongs to me. I am anything but a shriveled pea or a zombie bride. If I were to find a word to describe myself, it might even be beautiful. Beverly is not a speck in my mind now because I need to find Nolan. When I spin in front of the mirror, I realize I don't own a nice pair of shoes and I'm not about to slip my work ones back on. Maybe no one will notice a pair of raggedy flip-flops underneath all the ruffled fabric.

Hefting my backpack to my shoulders, I say, "Thanks for your help."

"You're walking?" I simply nod and Poh Poh shakes her head. "Outside." She tosses me a set of keys and my forehead wrinkles, not following what she's saying. Poh Poh walks me to the front door where a gold Vespa is parked outside. "My new ride. You like? Go. Jade will bring it home."

I start to refuse but walking up the cliff in these sandals, wearing this dress, and my backpack, would have me arriving at the B Hive feeling like a sweaty hunchback, and that's not the entrance I'd like to make. "Thank you."

If I didn't have a date with Nolan, I'd be tempted to drive the scooter around town for a while. I love the wind through my hair, so I take an extra lap down Lambert Avenue before driving up the hill because not being caged in while speeding down a road is an addicting feeling. If I were Nolan, and my dad left the keys in his motorcycle, I'd take it for an unauthorized ride too.

At the B Hive my hand brushes against the front door, but I can't pull it open. Not because it's locked, but because the excitement from trying on the dress and the ride up here is gone. I know Nolan is somewhere on the other side of this door, but so is Beverly. I shouldn't walk in. Something is bound to go wrong. The door pushes aside my anxiety when someone wearing a white button-down shirt opens it for me.

"The dining hall is filled with a bunch of old guys in suits and when they see you, there's a good chance someone's pacemaker is going to short circuit." My eyes snap up to Wick's smiling face and I'm flooded with relief, as if I'd been doing wall sits and was finally able to slump to the ground. He loops his arm through mine and as we take a step, he slides the tray he's balancing with his left hand in front of me. "Crabcake?"

"What are you doing?" I ask.

"I'm offering you a crabcake and you should take one, they're amazing," he says.

"No, what are you doing here?"

"Would you believe I'm offering everyone a crabcake? Seriously, take one before they are gone." I do and my eyes roll back. I haven't had anything this tasty in weeks. "I know. Seventh level of heaven good," Wick says. "My sister Alli makes them. She's catering tonight. Lacie and I are serving."

So, this is where Lacie is working tonight. I'll get to see her and thank her for the dress. My breathing calms as I walk with Wick. I expect him to escort me into the dining hall since his arm is still looped through mine, but we haven't started moving.

I take a step, but he won't budge. He whispers in my ear, "I think you're forgetting something."

My hands fly to my head. Did I somehow tie the bandana back over my hair? But it's not there. I smooth my dress down in front and back and all the fabric is where it should be. Other than forgetting reality, and Wick doesn't know about that, everything is fine.

Before I can ask what he is talking about, Wick tugs on the nylon strap of my backpack. I can't believe I almost forgot about my backpack. I don't even feel it anymore. Taking a few steps to reception, I stash it behind the desk while receiving a side-eye from Julian, the night manager.

Back at Wick's side my heart is pounding. "He'll have it sent to my room."

At that Wick loops his arm through mine again and we finally walk toward the dining room. Dodging that bullet was close, even closer than telling Nolan he couldn't pick me up at my room tonight because I needed to get the dress from Lacie, and I wanted to surprise him.

On a regular day, the dining room is beautiful, but tonight it's elegant. I helped hang the shimmery gold fabric that now flutters in front of the windows, but with the sun setting, and strategic lights aimed at the folds of fabric, it creates a dramatic backdrop. I'm in a dream, and not a floating through a cloud dream. It's more like the nightmare where you show up to school naked. My arm tightens on Wick's. Every day I walk into this building and slip on my housekeeping apron, instantly becoming invisible, but right now I am very exposed.

Heads turn as we pass and Wick elbows me in the side.

"They're drooling over your crabcakes," I say, gripping Wick's arm tighter, waiting for Beverly to appear.

He laughs. "Ease up on the death grip. I won't let them eat you, just the hors d'oeuvres. Promise, snack pack."

I try to laugh at Wick, but my chest is still tight. And then there is Nolan standing across the room. I finally come up for air. His back is to me and he's not wearing a jacket over his vest and dress shirt. The way his shoulders are held tight makes him look like he would rather be anywhere but here.

Wick makes a low whistle and Nolan turns.

Nolan's smile is the first snow of winter, soft with a hint of magic before becoming an all-consuming whiteout. Today, I don't mind when his eyes trace my silhouette. This is a much better situation than rainbow soft serve. I even give a half-turn when Wick releases me because Nolan is the only one standing in front of me.

If I *could* make my own tribe, I'd wish for Nolan to be the king. But I stopped making wishes long ago, because they never come true. Nolan doesn't say anything as he closes the distance between us, and before I have time to blink he slips his arm around my waist and kisses me. "You look amazing," he says. The words whisper across my skin before he kisses me again.

A cough followed by a squeal interrupts us. Wick punches Nolan in the shoulder and Lacie is practically jumping up and down. Nolan is at my side instead of in front of me, one arm glued around my waist as I reach behind my back, grabbing his other hand.

"I'm dead, I am actually dead right now. You're killing it," Lacie says, leaning forward, gently touching the fabric at my neck. "Do you like it?"

I let go of Nolan so I can give Lacie a real hug. "It's incredible. Thank you."

Her words brush against my ear. "Find me later. I need details about that kiss, because holy moly the fire alarm almost went off." She lets me go, snapping back into server mode, picking up the tray she set on a table. She makes a motion with her head toward the other guests and Wick follows her into the rotating collection of people.

"If I wasn't doing this for my mom, we'd leave right now," Nolan says. "I'd take you to Pedro's and it would only be the two of us." I don't hate the idea because as soon as Nolan mentioned his mom, my back stiffens and I have to resist the urge to run. Nolan wraps his arm around me again. "Maybe we'll go there after we stay the obligatory hour here. There's something I want to talk to you about."

The way he says this makes my heart race. Or it could be the kiss we just shared. Or the fact that his arm won't leave my side. Or the churning dread that I have to somehow avoid Beverly for an entire hour.

The gala is like a Rotary Club meeting on steroids. Rumbles of the same conversation float past as people mingle, everyone wonders how to improve Tinlee Bay, or how to attract a higher quality visitor to boost revenue.

Nolan's arm suddenly tightens around my waist. "Incoming," he warns as a man in a gray suit approaches us. "He's my dad's business partner."

"Nolan." The man's voice is expensive cologne, and he puts his hand out. Nolan shakes it quickly, returning his arm to my waist. The man keeps his palm extended in a greeting toward me. "Ben Hoffman." I shake his hand, before going back to the safety of holding Nolan's, but don't say anything, which seems to throw Ben off and he swivels his attention back to Nolan. "Calvin said you secured our latest acquisition. Said Peck and Company wouldn't have agreed to our offer if it wasn't for you. Hate to lose you in the fall, but at least it's to the likes of Berkeley."

Nolan's entire body tenses as he snorts. "Is that what my dad is telling you?"

Ben dismisses Nolan's question with a flick of his wrist. "Calvin understands cold feet." His voice drops. "He also knows his son is a chip off the old block and will do the right thing." Nolan is about to reply, when Ben says, "Speak of the devil."

Almost an exact replica of Nolan is headed toward us. Calvin isn't quite as tall as Nolan, and there's a smattering of gray at his temples, but father and son are carved from the same stone.

"Leave it to a Lambert to keep a beautiful woman all to himself," Calvin says, wielding his own hazardous smile like a sword.

Nolan almost crushes my hand in his. "Dad. Stop."

Ben slaps Calvin on the back and says, "I was telling Nolan how much he's going to enjoy the blue and the gold."

Nolan's words are clipped, his eyes locked with his dad. "And I was telling Ben that just because *you* say something doesn't mean it's true."

Calvin clears his throat, locking his eyes on mine. "We've not met."

Before I can answer, a familiar voice slides past my right

shoulder. "My favorite people all standing together. Except for you, of course, Benjamin."

Calvin, Ben, and Beverly laugh as I become the one clenching Nolan's hand. This cannot be happening. What should I do? Nolan's gaze burns the side of my face, but there's no time to run away. Beverly kisses Calvin's cheek, looping her arm through his as she turns to face Nolan.

"Great timing," Calvin says. "Our son was about to introduce me to his friend."

My mouth goes dry, and my armpits start sweating as Beverly places her full attention on whoever her son has draped on his arm. Me. This is it. Anything I say will expose the list of lies I've strung together.

I've never been more thankful for Nolan to speak first. "Rindy, these are my parents. Mom, Dad, this is my girlfriend, Rindy."

What? I choke on the saliva I've managed to accumulate in my desert mouth, but my heart is still walking a tightrope. My head whips to Nolan, I still can't say anything. All I can do is stare into his blue eyes, which are as bright as stars burning against the night sky.

In the field at the end of Sylvia's property, there was a simple metal gate that always stuck when I tried to open it. But I learned the trick: you had to press the latch and give it a shake for the metal to release. Every time after that, when I slid my thumb over the latch, it felt like I was coming home because I was lucky enough to be in on the secret.

When Nolan called me his girlfriend a gate in my heart

swung open. For a moment everything fades, and it's only Nolan and me. Beverly and Calvin might as well have disappeared.

Nolan's mouth is at my ear. "Are you okay? Say something. I wanted to talk to you about this later tonight."

The three people standing with us have no idea what is happening between Nolan and I. They have no idea that this is a revelation to me. Girlfriend. Another title I've never worn. I can't believe how easily the word rolled off Nolan's tongue, like he'd been waiting to say it.

"Will you be joining Nolan at Berkeley in the fall?" Calvin asks me.

I tear my eyes off Nolan's face, lifting my chin even though I'm scared, not defiant. "No."

Nolan offers the truth he knows. "Rindy's from Montana, she's been vacationing here this summer."

Beverly coughs. It sounds like a perfectly ordinary cough, but I caught her eye. She would be an exceptionally good poker player. Her face holds the same neutral smile as when she joined the circle. I want to wipe my sweaty hands down the front of my dress. How can she stand there keeping her face free from any reaction?

Ben grabs a glass of wine off a tray from a server that isn't Wick or Lacie. "Missoula or Bozeman then?"

Ben doesn't mean to irritate me with his comment, but he does. I met a girl at camp one summer, and late one night neither of us could sleep so we snuck down to dip our feet in the lake. I told her I didn't know who my parents were but all she did was shrug and say, "So what if you're adopted." I loved and hated her for that. I loved that it wasn't a big deal to her, but I hated that she assumed everyone gets adopted.

"Neither. I'm not going to university." When I say this, Calvin raises an arm in a gesture that seems to say, "*great, another one,*" then he grabs a wine glass for himself and one for Beverly. "College isn't an option for everyone," I say, "and even if it was, it's not the only choice." Nolan squeezes my hip in reassurance, for which I'm thankful because I can't believe I said that to his dad.

Calvin takes a sip and then says, "Maybe not the only choice, but clearly a notch above the rest. There is no denying the opportunities a degree gives a person."

Nolan takes a slight step forward. "Dad, drop it. You're disappointed in me. Don't take it out on Rindy."

Calvin shakes his head. "I'm not taking it out on anyone. I'm simply stating facts."

My ears are ringing, almost drowning out Beverly's question. "What will you do in the fall, Rindy?"

When Beverly says my name, it's laced with familiarity, and why wouldn't it be? She signs my paycheck every two weeks. I feel like someone stepped on my heart, stopping it, but then it beats with a wallop against my ribs. "Work."

I let go of Nolan's hand and twist the ends of my hair, but I realize what I'm doing and my hand flops down at my side. Nolan grabs it once again, anchoring me to himself. One simple word is the most I can manage without revealing to

Nolan that I already have a job. I stare at Beverly, offering a few mute blinks: please let me still have a job.

Beverly's eyebrow ticks up, an almost invisible movement, but I see it and my brain interprets it into a thousand different meanings, and none of them seem good.

Calvin drains the rest of his wine. "Where will—"

"Cal, I think we've taken up enough of their time, don't you?" Beverly asks.

Calvin glances at his wife and whatever secret look she gives him works because he turns back to us, his saber smile glinting. "Yes, of course."

They leave and I am shaking enough that Nolan feels it and pulls me to his chest. "I'm so sorry. I'd like to say they aren't always like this, but they are. My dad enjoys showing off when he meets someone new." Nolan's eyes are suddenly desperate. "It's not because of what I said, is it? I've been waiting to talk to you. Is this too much? Too soon?"

Nolan takes a breath to say something else, but I reach out, putting the palm of my hand against his stubble. All of a sudden my body stops shaking. I haven't told Nolan the absolute truth, about anything, but right now I can. "It's not too much. It's perfect." This time I'm the one leaning forward, kissing him.

It's a long time before we stop, and he leans his forehead against mine. "Let's get out of here."

I squeeze his hand, and he kisses me again before leading me toward the far exit. As we walk, the hair on my arms stands up. A glance over my shoulder reveals Beverly watching my every move. I almost trip over the hem of my dress. Did she see us kissing? I pull to a stop, grabbing a glass of what I hope is water off a serving tray, draining it, and returning the glass before we disappear out the door. I don't want to know what Beverly is thinking or what will happen in the morning when she isn't a poised, expressionless gala host, but once again my boss.

22

I don't normally stop by the dining room on my way to the supply closet, but this morning I do. I'm curious if the shimmery gold fabric is still strung in front of the windows. It's not, and I wonder who took it down. Every last reminder of the gala is gone. Maybe last night didn't happen at all? I press my fingers to my lips, keeping the smile from overtaking me. Right there, where a small round table with a white linen tablecloth is housing two pitchers of orange juice and a carafe of coffee, is where Nolan called me his girlfriend.

I'm not sure how that's even possible. Why does he want me? No one has ever wanted me. I rip open the protein bar that I'm going to hate every bite of. I don't even get it out of the wrapper before Beverly appears at my side and my appetite vanishes.

"Surely we can do better than that," she says. The way she looks at me longer than necessary makes me wonder if she's talking about my face and not my breakfast. I can't keep eye contact with her and steal a glance back into the dining room, scanning for the ghost of Nolan with his arm around me, and I know Beverly saw us. I bite my lip. No doubt, Beverly would prefer if my face was far, far away from his.

"Follow me," she says and I'm not about to disobey. We bypass the dining room and enter through the kitchen staff entrance at the end of the hall. Beverly tucks a stack of papers under her arm. "She needs a plate," Beverly says.

A hairnetted cook glances over his shoulder with a quick nod. "Sure thing."

Beverly smiles at him. "When you're finished, please come to my office." She leaves without a backward glance.

The cook hands me a plate piled high with scrambled eggs and bacon, a slice of toast resting on the top. "Last meal?" He winks with a smile, revealing a silver-capped tooth. When I don't immediately grab the plate he says, "Go on. I'll just have to toss it otherwise."

My stomach grumbles. Picturing all that food dumped in the trash convinces me to take it. If this is my last meal I might as well lick the plate clean, which is pretty much what I do. I won't lie, having a stomach full of a freshly cooked breakfast is a wonderful thing. Much better than the brick of protein I ingest every day.

I'd spend the rest of the morning hanging out in this corner of the kitchen, but Beverly probably knows exactly how long it should take a person to eat a plate of food. If I don't turn up soon, it could be one more reason she wants to fire me. My breakfast threatens to reappear. I have to keep my job. I've never been called to her office before, and why else would the cook say this is my last meal? Maybe the cook has seen Beverly do this before? I rub my sweating hands on the linen towel before setting that and the empty plate on the counter—I need to find a way to convince Beverly to let me keep my job. But I have no idea how to do that.

Beverly's voice slides under the closed door of her office, but I knock anyway. There's a pause before she tells me to enter, and when I do, she has her phone to her ear. She mouths *sorry* while pointing to the empty chair. Then she turns to the wall, not missing a beat in her conversation.

It's hard not to eavesdrop, but the phone calls sounds like a replica of every conversation swirling the room last night. I turn my attention to the ginormous family photo. How old was Nolan? Five? Eight? I wish I could see his face. Did he already know Lacie was his sister? I never asked how he found out, or how old he was when he did. Details like that don't matter when the truth you uncover is a landmine, but now I wish I knew.

Beverly's chair protests as she swings back to her desk. "Sorry, my phone has been ringing all morning." As if to showcase that fact, it rings again and Beverly silences it, turning it face down on her desk. Briefly pressing her fingertips to her temples, she says, "Did Nolan tell you we had a bid for Ivy & Goose to come to town? Do you know what that is?"

Heat runs up my back at the sound of Nolan's name, but I shake my head.

I've never played chess, but we had some heated Connect Four tournaments at Gov's. Sometimes a girl could get so lost in the moves she was planning that she couldn't see the obvious move right in front of her, and her opponent would make the same face Beverly does right now because she knew she was going to win.

"Have you been to Malibu?" When I shake my head again, Beverly says, "I didn't think so. Ivy & Goose is *the* restaurant right now, and they have been looking to expand. The clientele they attract is exactly what we want. It will allow us to launch Tinlee Bay into another bracket." Beverly clicks her tongue against her teeth. "But they backed out."

I should contribute something, and maybe if I manage to keep the conversation centered on Ivy & Goose there's a chance Beverly will forget why she asked me to come here in the first place. "Maybe it's for the best," I say.

There's a lift to the corner of Beverly's mouth. "Not one for change?"

Every time one of my placements was about to end it always put me in a strange no-man's-land. I no longer belonged to that foster family, not like I ever felt like I belonged inside their house anyway, but knowing I only had two days left always filled me with a strange sense of courage to speak my mind. If my time here is coming to an end, I might as well go for it. "I never said that. But I don't think you need Ivy & Goose. Why only appeal to a small percentage of people when you have the uniqueness of Tinlee Bay at your doorstep? Everyone, regardless of their status"—I flick my eye from the tip of my shoes up to Beverly's eyes—"can enjoy that."

Beverly slips her glasses on, making a note. "Go on."

Go on? Like I'm here to give my *How-to-Improve-Tinlee-Bay-TED-Talk*. Except if I'm convincing enough, maybe I can save my job? The problem is, I don't have anything else to say. Reaching for my hair, I turn and twist it, and as I do, I know what to say.

"If you want Tinlee Bay to shine, highlight what makes this place amazing. The people. They make it amazing." I push Nolan out of my thoughts because I don't want to start talking about him. My mind turns to Lacie's family. "Invite Jade to give specialized yoga lessons to your guests. Or offer coupons for her studio." Beverly's champion Connect Four face morphs into her expressionless poker face and I almost fall out of my chair. What am I doing? Why did I mention Jade, the woman Calvin had an affair with? I'd be safer telling Beverly how much I love kissing her son than to keep talking about Jade. I rush ahead before Beverly sees the terror in my eyes and wonders why. "Local artists. Create one-of-a-kind pop-up events. Something like what Wick's sister does with Alli Cats."

I snap my fingers at another idea. "You should have your own apiary. People love buying local, plus 'save the bees, save the trees,' right? What would be better than bringing home a jar of B Hive honey from your vacation? What Tinlee Bay needs is already right here."

Beverly writes another note, then leans back in her chair, her fingertips pressed together in a triangle shape. "How did you meet my son?"

I unravel my twisted hair and start again. This must be what a gazelle feels like after the lion has worn it down and is about to devour it. I'm not stupid, she called Nolan *her son* just then to remind me he belongs to her. The air whooshes out of my mouth. "There was a bonfire." I leave everything else out, like how I didn't have a place to live so why not wander the beach alone in the middle of the night and lie to everyone I met?

She nods. "I can see why he likes you."

I snort so hard I grab a tissue from the box at the corner of her desk and wipe my face in case I sprayed spit all over my lip. I don't understand what Beverly is doing. First, she feeds me, then she lets me blabber on about Tinlee Bay, and now we're talking about Nolan. She keeps talking. "It's not anyone who can speak their mind to Calvin like you did last night." Beverly pauses and I twist the Kleenex in my hands. Is that a compliment? It doesn't feel like a compliment. It feels like hot lion breath on my back and I squirm in my seat. "Between last night and this morning, I've spoken to everyone on the city council, and no one has had a single good idea about how to pivot from the setback of losing out on Ivy & Goose. And you"—she glances at her paper—"just gave me three off the top of your head."

Pivoting from setbacks. If nothing else, that could be the epitaph on my grave. I've been doing exactly that my entire life. I pinch my lips together because I have no idea what Beverly will say next, and I don't want to be smiling if she is about to fire me.

Beverly leans down, opens a drawer, and pulls out a small stack of cards bound together with a blue rubber band. "Do you know what these are?"

I do in fact know what they are. They are comment cards that are left in every room and stacked at reception.

"How long have you worked here?" Beverly asks.

I can see a flash of lion's teeth coming in for the kill. This is why I was called into her office in the first place.

"Three months," I say, wishing I had a water bottle; it's suddenly hard to swallow. I rack my mind for a time when Mina warned me about complaints, sure there have been some difficult guests, but I don't think anyone has been dissatisfied with my work.

Beverly nods and the ends of her bob sway. "I read all the cards. Some have a comment or suggestion. Most tend to be bored kids exercising vocabulary skills their parents would be embarrassed by." She removes the rubber band. "The sad truth is that it's not very often a person takes the time to write something kind on one of these." She locks her Nolan-look-alike eyes on mine. "But when they do, these are the cards I keep." She sets the stack on her desk, scooting it toward me.

I read some about Mina and a few about Joslyn in reception. The rest have employee names I don't recognize and figure they were here before my time. Then I get to one with my name on it from the guy who lost his slippers and claimed he never had the right tea packets in his room. Then another one from a mom who thanked me for finding her daughter's stuffed animal that got folded into the sleeper couch.

I set the cards on Beverly's desk, still unsure where she is going with all of this.

"I underestimated you. Housekeeping is anything but glamorous, but two cards in three months has me sitting up to take notice. I want you to know that I see your hard work and as a result, I'm giving you a very generous raise to ensure I can keep you here at the B Hive."

My jaw swings open and before I start drooling on her desk, I clamp it closed. Getting a raise was not even something I considered. I haven't really missed having a phone, but I want it right now. I want to whip it out and call Nolan to tell him the good news. Then I'd call every house I ever lived in and tell them I'm not a failure. In fact, I am generous raise material.

My mouth starts moving as fast as my thoughts. "Thank you. Thank you. Thank you. You have no idea what this means. This means everything to me." I push the tangled twist of hair I created over my shoulder while sitting up a little taller in the chair. "Thank you. I won't let you down."

Beverly takes off her glasses, smiling at me, and it feels like she is about to say *connect four, I win*. Instead, she says, "No, I don't think you will."

23

Hector is already stocked, and my list of assigned rooms waits on top, along with a butterscotch candy which is normally the sweetest thing of my morning, but not today. I still can't believe Beverly gave me a raise. This is exactly what I need: it pushes me closer to finding a place to live. I don't trust myself to start cleaning rooms until I release some of the energy crashing through my body. If I don't, I might accidentally short-sheet the bed, or completely forget to scrub the toilet. I need to talk to someone. The B Hive is only so big, and it doesn't take long to find Norma parked outside a room. Inside, Mina is bent over the clawfoot tub like a giraffe at a watering hole.

It doesn't matter that I've been pretending not to notice her in the hall as we pass, or that I can't fully explain my sky-high level of excitement. I need to tell someone. "Mina, I got a raise!"

The spray bottle clatters to the bottom of the tub and Mina jerks up, gloved hand clutching her chest. "Lands alive, Rindy, it's too early in the morning to give me a heart attack." She takes a deep breath, releasing it slowly out her mouth. "Now, say that again, this time without almost killing me."

"I got a raise." I spin a circle. "I thought Beverly was going to fire me. But she gave me a raise." I clamp my hands on Mina's shoulders. "Do you know what this means?" I don't wait for an answer. "This means I can finally find a place to liv—"

I let go of Mina and back away. I got carried away and wasn't careful with what I said, and it's like I plugged in a neon sign because the word I stopped myself from saying blinks to life, glowing between Mina and I.

Mina brushes a coiled curl out of her face, but it springs right back. Her words are slow and carefully chosen. "Rindy, where have you been living all this time?"

Taking another step back, I swat the air as if I spritzed too much of the lemon verbena air freshener we use. "It doesn't matter. None of that matters, don't you see? Everything is fine."

Mina gently takes hold of my still-waving wrist. "I'm glad everything is fine, but I'm guessing it hasn't been for a while. Has it?" Her thoughtful question sinks into my bones, a weight reminding me of my truth.

She lets go and I clasp my hands behind my back to keep them still. "It doesn't matter." I don't know what else to say without telling her everything, and I'm not ready to do that.

Once I have the key to my new place firmly in hand then maybe I'll tell her.

Mina sighs before a small smile appears. "I'm happy you're happy." But she doesn't look happy. I don't know what else to do so I let her go back to scrubbing and leave to get Hector. I no longer feel like I'm about to rattle loose from excitement, but I'm not sure I feel better for telling Mina my news. She doesn't understand how much this means to me.

Beverly's words play on a loop in my mind as I finish my second room. *A significant raise.* I don't know what that means, but it will be significantly better than a canoe. Maybe I can ask Ronda in HR, that way I can start to plan. The idea of having enough money to turn my phone back on, eat anything besides protein bars, and not sleep on the ground lifts the weight of the world off my shoulders. This raise is the lifeline I've needed. Excitement bubbles in my chest, flowing to my head, making me dizzy. I trip over my own feet and accidentally dump the stack of towels I'm carrying. I refold them only to knock all the tiny bottles of shampoo off the top of Hector as well. My excitement is starting to pry me open again. I wish I could talk to Nolan.

Running my dust rag across the bedside table, I lift the phone off the surface and swipe under it, and before I can stop myself I pick up the receiver, press nine, and dial Nolan's number which I've had memorized since he gave it to me the afternoon we went to the lighthouse, in case I wanted to break my technology fast, he had said with a wink.

It goes straight to voicemail which is a relief to my pounding heart because suddenly I'm worried the room will be charged for this call.

"Hey, it's me." I twist my finger through the cord. "Anyway. I have something amazing to tell you and I really want to see you. Meet me by the shaved ice stand at 4:30." There are several ways I could end the call. *Can't wait. See you soon. I love you.* My breath catches. Do I? Am I in love with Nolan? I don't know the answer so I hang up without saying anything else.

By the time I arrive, Nolan is already sitting on the back of a bench along the promenade, his sandaled feet planted on the slats meant for sitting, his elbows on his knees, watching the ocean. What will it be like for him to leave all this behind? I can't imagine turning my back on this view, especially now that it's mine, and I bounce on my toes. After this morning's talk with Beverly, Tinlee Bay really is mine, and with the added income I'll be able to find a place to live sooner than I expected.

I slide up to Nolan, bumping my shoulder into his. "Hey," I say.

His shoulders tense but when he sees it's me, he relaxes, a smile spreading like wildfire across his face. "Hey yourself."

I'm glad I'm not wearing my Smokey the Bear shirt because the fire of his smile is not something I want to extinguish. He scoots over so I can sit next to him, and he drapes his arm across my back. "I'm glad you called, I have something I wanted to tell you too." He leans his mouth to my ear. "I'm glad you embraced technology long enough to call me. If you need me to, I'll apologize on your behalf to your parents. That is, if you want me to meet them."

I jump off the bench again, but the playfulness in Nolan's eyes is teetering toward confusion so I sit back down and pull a knot out of my hair. My stomach is in more knots than my hair at the mention of my nonexistent parents. I swallow the rising lump and ignore his attempt to get me to agree that meeting good old Mom and Dad would be a good idea. "You wanted to tell me something, so you go first."

Nolan's arm tightens across my back with a gentle squeeze. "Nope. I've been waiting all day to hear what you have to say."

As much as I love being next to Nolan, I have too much uncontained energy to sit still. Leaping off the back of the bench for the second time, I take a few pacing steps in front of him repeating the word *job* and not *raise* in my mind to ensure I say the right thing, then clasp my hands together at my chest as I face him. "I got a job!"

The fire of his smile fades, his blue eyes as wide as the endless Pacific behind me. "You what?"

I stammer a little. "I got a job. A good one. Enough to let me stay here. Permanently." Tears sting the corners of my eyes, but I blink them away. I've waited my whole life to have *permanently placed* stamped on my file and it never happened. Not until today. Not until I made it happen with my own hard work. Nolan stretches his arms out, grabbing my hands in his, his thumb almost rubbing a patch of skin off my knuckles. I can tell he's forcing his smile not to slip.

He's quiet, too quiet. "Say something," I whisper.

The crashing waves coupled with squeals from excited children are louder than Nolan's voice. "This job. This is what you want?"

I'm about to tell Nolan that I want this more than anything, but the words dissolve into thin air. It's like not knowing how to end the phone call earlier. Staying here is exactly what I want. Moving to Tinlee Bay. Finding a job. Having a place to live. Security. Knowing I can make it on my own. I set my sights on this happening a year ago and sure, it hasn't gone according to plan, but today is the first time I've taken a breath without being afraid.

I still haven't answered his question. Being homeless was never part of my plan. Neither was meeting Nolan. I need a place to live more than anything and nod several times. "This is what I want." My answer sounds weak.

His smile is pinched as he hops off the bench and wraps me in his arms. "I'm happy for you." But his voice sounds as thin as mine. Like we are reciting lines in a play neither of us wants to be in.

Mina's happiness didn't sound convincing either. In order for both Mina or Nolan to understand the level of relief and excitement I feel right now, they would have to know the depth of everything I've been through. It hurts keeping myself walled off from Nolan. But I can't tell him the truth. Not when I'm so close to finally achieving everything I need. He plans on leaving Tinlee Bay, and sooner or later, he'll wake up to the fact that I'm not who he wants. Everyone always does. I only have right now, so I lean my head into his shoulder, taking a deep breath. Nolan smells like leftover campfire, tree sap, and the breeze off the ocean, everything that I love. I try to clear my mind but only manage to clear my throat with something that sounds like a cough. "What did you want to tell me?" I ask.

At first, I'm not sure he hears me, but he lets out a breath. "It doesn't matter." His voice cracked as his eyes darkened. He rests his chin on the top of my head, releasing another long exhale. "I was going to ask you to come with me when I leave." At that, I pull myself out of his arms and he cradles my face in his hands. "I thought we could be together."

His words are a knife through my heart. The fire has gone out of his eyes, they smolder under a wet sheen that I refuse to believe is the start of tears. This doesn't happen in my life. People don't cry over me, they always let me go. I've always been the one left alone digging a palm into my eyes trying to keep the tears from falling. Not the other way around.

This is why I never wanted to learn how to swim because now I know what drowning feels like. I'm finally getting the security I've been working so hard to gain for myself, and now Nolan wants me to leave that all behind and go with him. I press my face back into the crook of his arm. He was so calm and reassuring when we stood in his pool, when he told me he would never hurt me. I believed him because I knew it was true. But deep down I always knew this would also be true: I would be the one to end up hurting him.

24

The rest of the week is a blur. As I clean every room, I force myself not to think about Nolan and the fact that he wants me to leave with him in a few weeks. I haven't been able to sleep because of it. What would it be like to say yes? There would be hours of endless roads stretching out in front of us with nothing but each other for company—but leaving with him is a risk I cannot take. The worst that can happen to Nolan is all his plans crumble at his feet and he slinks back home, tail between his legs. The worst that can happen to me is my life on repeat, being abandoned at a gas station in the middle of nowhere with a *sorry this didn't work out, maybe someday it will all make sense.*

I'm finished with my last room of the day and am about to close the door when my eyes flick to the phone on the bedside table. I should call Nolan and tell him we need to talk. But everything I need to say is locked inside my heart, so

I pull the door closed and put Hector away. After that, I practically run to pick up my paycheck.

I have no idea what a significant raise amounts to, but I'm about to find out. I hardly get the envelope out of Ronda's hand before I tear it open. I'm not breathing, and it's not from the raise, which is indeed significant. It's from another check inside the envelope with a note paperclipped to it. *This is a one-time bonus, letting you know how pleased I am you are staying here with everything you love. — Beverly.*

Everything I love. How does Beverly know what that is?

Ronda jokes she is part reptile because she keeps this cubicle of an office stifling hot, even still a chill runs down my spine. If I were to light a match right now and hold it underneath this note, Beverly's invisible message would appear. She assumes I love Nolan and that if I stay in Tinlee Bay, so will he. Which is probably what she wants so she and Calvin can convince him to go to Berkeley. In all my daydreaming about going with Nolan, I never once pictured him staying in Tinlee Bay.

If I asked him, would he stay here—with me? Would it be wrong to try?

Before I could dare, I need to make sure I have something other than a canoe. I walk back to Ronda's desk. "Could I borrow your phone for a second?" I'm ready with an easy lie about how I forgot mine, but she only smiles with a nod.

Lacie answers on the second ring. "Hello?"

"Hey, it's me," I say.

"Hey, chica. It's your lucky day I answered because most of the time it's a hard pass. What's up?"

I take a deep breath. "Do you want to help me look for an apartment?"

I swear even Ronda scoots back from her desk at the sound of Lacie's scream through the receiver.

My ear is still ringing by the time I meet Lacie at her house. The door is barely open before she starts talking. "Okay. I did some searching, and not going to lie, there are not many good options. There's one down the road and the lady said if we could be there within the hour, she'd be around to show it to us." She waves her hands at me, shooing me back down the steps.

The apartment is a fully furnished converted garage. It's all one open room. A bed calls to me from the back corner. All I want to do is fling myself on it and bury my head in the pillows. I could fall asleep here. I could lie on my stomach and doomscroll as soon as I turn my phone back on. I could dream of Nolan on that bed. The temperature in the room seems to rise several degrees as the woman points to the kitchen lining one side wall. This is where I could ask Nolan what his favorite meal is and make it for him. Lacie grabs my hand, pulling me past the couch and table in the front of the room where I could curl up next to Nolan as we watch something on TV. Lacie pulls me into the bathroom, revealing a shower/tub combo, toilet, sink, and a stackable washer/dryer unit. These are simply the basics, but I might as well have died and gone to heaven.

The woman crosses her arms at her chest as she finishes a run-through of details I'm only half listening to—because all I want is Nolan in this apartment with me. "I've had a few other people asking to view it, but you're the first, so if you're serious, get back to me as soon as you can and the place is yours," the woman says.

I'm scraping my foot over the line of grout in between tiles on the floor and don't acknowledge the woman. There is nothing to think about. This place is fully furnished, and if I wanted to, I could take a shower and do laundry at the same time. But I can't make myself say anything. If I can't convince Nolan to stay, will Beverly demand I pay back the bonus? Could I lose my raise, or worse, my job if Nolan doesn't want to stay? I can't come this close to everything I need only to have it pulled out from under me. Before I met up with Lacie, I stopped at the bank to cash the checks in case Beverly came to her senses, realizing the mistake she made by giving me this bonus, but now the money burns in my back pocket.

"Earth to Rindy." Lacie clears her throat, turning to my would-be-landlady. "Could we have a minute?" Lacie asks. As soon as the woman leaves through the front door, Lacie pounces. "Why are you not jumping up and down? This place is perfect. If I wasn't forced to live at home, I'd want a place exactly like this."

Being forced to live at home with an amazing mom and a slightly scary grandmother is not a bad option in life. Lacie doesn't know how lucky she is, and her annoyance at my hesitation turns sour in my stomach. I try to ignore it because she's right, this place is amazing.

Stepping closer, I run a finger along the countertop. "Of course I'll take it. I just wish I had someone I could talk this through with instead of doing it on my own."

"You could talk to your boyfriend." Lacie makes kissy lips at me. "You still haven't told me about that five-alarm kiss Nolan gave you at the gala." She shakes her hand like she touched the burner of a stove. "I've been so jealous of you. Curves that will not quit, the best guy in the world looking at you like he wants to eat you." She spins. "This place! Are your parents paying for this? You are seriously having the best summer."

Of course, she thinks I don't have a care in the world. I'm here on vacation with parents who supposedly love me, wandering the beach in a haze and falling for the man of my dreams. I pull my shoulders back, jutting my jaw. I'm not a hundred percent sure Nolan is my boyfriend after what happened. And I don't want to consult him, I want to surprise him with the fact that I have a place to live, then ask if he wants to stay. But when I imagine asking Nolan, it feels like an elephant is sitting on my chest. How could he choose between me and the endless open road that he's been dreaming of?

Lacie reads my tense posture. "Uh-oh, you can't be having problems with Nolan already. I need you to calm him down, he's mad at me."

I'm guessing it's me that Nolan is mad at, not Lacie, and I try to let some of my annoyance escape by latching on to this new thread of a conversation. "How come?" I ask.

Lacie joins me at the bathroom counter, leaning as close to the mirror as she can before putting her face in mine. "Do you see this?" She pulls down her right eyelid. "There's a speck of green in my eye. See it?"

Lacie is so close that I need to step back so I can focus. Sure enough, at the bottom of her iris, there is a tiny slice of green.

She releases her finger and leans back to the mirror while she talks. "I've always wondered who my dad is." She stops talking and I know what she's doing as she examines her face. She's mining it for clues, wondering if she could peel back her features to find her father. It's something I've done a thousand times. She takes a breath. "I don't know why I never thought of this until now but the other day it hit me, I bet he has green eyes." Lacie pushes off the counter, spinning to face me again. "I told all this to Nolan. Told him I'm going to do one of those DNA tests and he freaked out. I have never seen him get so mad."

As Lacie keeps talking, the truth of who Lacie's father is simmers inside the pot of my fear that Nolan would not choose me if I asked him to.

"Anyway. Can you please talk some sense into him? Calm him down. Explain that this is no big deal, that he doesn't need to protect me from whatever he thinks I'll find."

She waves her hand in front of her as if she's erasing everything she said. "But that's me. Drama. Let's get back to you and your perfect life, and your perfect boyfriend, and this perfect apartment."

Each time Lacie ticks something off the list from my so-called perfect life, I take a step closer to the edge of the cliff. I need to take a breath and calm down, but I can't. My heart rate increases with every breath I take. Beverly paid me to convince Nolan to stay in Tinlee Bay, and I have the cash to prove it along with a list of doubts that he'd ever agree. Nolan wants me to leave everything I've worked for and go with him. Lacie wants me to convince Nolan that a DNA test is no big deal. Why won't he just tell her the truth? My heart feels like it's been slammed into a brick wall. Why haven't I told Nolan the truth? I'm exhausted from keeping all these secrets stuffed inside my heart. I'm exhausted from holding myself together.

The simmering pot of my emotions boils over. "Nolan is protecting you from the truth because that's what a brother should do!" I shout.

It takes several seconds for what I said to register in Lacie's brain, but when it does her eyes widen in disbelief. "What did you say?"

I cover my face with my hands. I have to walk this back to safer waters. "Like a brother. I meant Nolan acts like a brother to you." I can't take my hands off my face because I don't want to see the look Lacie must be giving me. Nolan's disappointed face, the one he gave me last night, flashes in my mind. He'll never choose to stay with me even if I asked. Especially not after this.

I don't have to remove my hands to know that Lacie is crying, but I do. She is full-on cannot-catch-her-breath sobbing and I stand there watching her because I don't know what else to do. "I know how you must feel," I say.

Lacie swipes a hand across her face, her lungs shuddering. "Don't stand there and talk to me about what I'm feeling." She takes a breath to maybe shout something else, but turns and runs from the bathroom instead, the blue tips of her hair swinging across her back, the door slamming behind her.

I stagger to the ledge of the tub and lean against it. What have I done? If Nolan was frustrated with me before, he'll be furious with me now. I can't undo this.

There's a knock on the door and the woman pokes her head into the bathroom, scanning the room, maybe half expecting to find the mirror shattered on the ground. "I got another call from someone wanting to view—"

I've screwed everything up, but I will not screw this up. I will not lose out on having a place to live. I don't know how to fix things with Lacie, or Nolan, or if either would want me to. Three months of sleeping on the ground has been long enough, and I can't let what's happened ruin my chance at finally having a place to live.

"Do you have a lease agreement with you?" The woman

nods. "Great." I reach into my pocket, pulling out a folded wad of bills. "First and last month?" Seeing the stack of cash in my hand seals the deal and I follow her into the main room to sign the paperwork. Before I can appreciate what's happening, she hands me the key to my very own house.

25

The loudest sound you'll ever hear is an empty apartment. I have everything I worked for. Wall-to-wall plank flooring. A deadbolt. A skylight in the bathroom that I didn't notice earlier. It's all mine, but I've never felt so alone. Twenty-four hours ago, I would have told you that I had nothing. No security, an uncertain future, not even a roof over my head or the ability to take a shower or use the toilet when needed.

I don't even want to take a hot shower right now. Having a place of my own should feel like a victory, but it doesn't. Instead, it fills me with the same weak-legged tingly sensation as right before you throw up. I need to lie down. I don't know what time it is; there's still light out the window but I must have fallen asleep, because the next thing I know it's pitch-black and someone is pounding on my door.

I jump off the bed, heart thumping along with the banging. The pounding continues, this time accompanied by

Nolan's voice. "Open the door, Rindy." Turning on the light, I walk over and open the front door. I'm about to ask how he knew I was here, even though I know the answer. Lacie is the only person who could have told him.

Nolan pushes past me. "How could you? How could you tell Lacie like that? I trusted you." His hair is sticking out at all angles like he's been pulling on it all night.

"I never asked you to trust me." I should have said something else, anything would have been better than that.

Nolan makes a strange sound. "Wow. Okay." He drops to the couch, leaning forward, holding his head in his hands.

He has shown me nothing but kindness, even the beginning flickering of love, and betraying his trust is how I repay him. I want to go to him and hold his hand, but I've lost the right to do that, so I clasp my own hands together behind my back.

Nolan lifts his head and it's the first time tonight I've seen his eyes; they are a bloodshot mess. "Tell me why you did it."

For the same reason I've done everything in my life: to protect myself when I felt threatened. I don't have a brother or a father or a mother to do it for me, and I was so sick of hearing what Lacie thought of my life, how perfect it seemed to her through the sheen of all the freshly painted lies I've shown her.

"I was upset," I say, a sorry shorthand version of the truth I'm unequipped to reveal.

Nolan is quiet for a long time, but I can feel the anger

radiating off his skin like a fresh sunburn. "This changes everything," he says.

At first, I assume he's talking about whatever our relationship is now, but in the silence, the weight of what I did settles on my shoulders. It's only a matter of time before Beverly and Calvin find out that Lacie knows the truth. What about Jade? She must have kept the truth from Lacie for a reason.

Nolan stands up, coming over to where I've stood, too afraid to try to reach out to him. He lifts a section of my tangled hair in his fingers. "How can I be so angry with you and still want to wrap my arms around you?" he asks.

My stomach tightens. "You shouldn't. I ruin everything."

He doesn't deny it because now he has firsthand knowledge of how true that is. But he hasn't let go of my hair. The air in the apartment shifts. Nolan is still angry, I can feel it, but there's another emotion pulsing off his skin, sadness, or maybe desperation. "I can't get you out of my mind. Not since the first time I met you." Nolan winds his hand through my hair until his palm is hot against my neck and I want to lean my whole body into his hand. "Come with me," he says.

Nolan's voice is a whisper. It's a plea. It's agony.

I'm afraid to move. How can he say that after I pulled the pin on a grenade and threw it into his life? Why would he be willing to let his anger settle to the ground so quickly? I let my lungs finally expand and I lean into his hand one more time before he removes it because I know he will when I say this. "You could stay in Tinlee Bay."

"I can't do that." His hand slips off my skin. "I thought you understood why I need to leave."

I understand that more than he'll ever know.

He leans his forehead against mine, waiting for me to say something, but I don't trust myself to say anything else. "I wish this wasn't happening," he says.

I used to light matches to see if I could feel the universe shift underneath me, revealing the day I was born so I could have another clue as to who I am. I used to wander into the tall grass at the end of Gov's property in the middle of the night, hunting the sky for shooting stars to wish for a family. All I've ever wanted is to have a place where I could unpack and not be forced to shove my belongings into a trash bag before moving along to yet another foster family.

And now I finally have that. I can finally set my back-pack down and stay.

I breathe Nolan in, memorizing the smell of fire, trees, and wind that clings to his shirt. I wish this wasn't happening either, but wishes are for people who believe they'll come true, and I stopped believing a long time ago.

"You should go," I say.

It's the last thing I want Nolan to do, but I need him to leave because having him stand in front of me, asking me to go with him, is breaking me in half. He shoves both hands through his hair as if he's deciding on something, then he pulls me to his chest. He hesitates for an instant and I see a flash in his eyes, a spark that could set the whole world on fire. Then his lips cover mine. The kiss is a tidal wave that sweeps me into his current, but the storm of his emotions break and the sea turns rugged. When it is over, I wrap my arms around my middle, alone and breathless, crashed against the rocks of this storm.

Nolan doesn't raise his eyes to find mine one last time, or run his hand through his hair, or say anything else. He simply walks away, closing the door behind him.

26

I pace around the edges of my apartment, past the couch to the bed, past the kitchen, and back to the couch. Every lap adds another line to the list in my head. *How could you do this? Tell me why? Come with me.* It's a treadmill I can't get off. I keep circling the room and before I know it the sun has warmed the sky. I head to work in the same clothes I wore yesterday.

"Morning," Mina calls as I enter the supply room, but I ignore her as I grab a stack of fitted sheets to throw onto Hector. Mina hands me my list of rooms and I yank it from her grasp.

"Nice to see you're in such a good mood this morning," Mina says.

I'm operating on zero sleep and a freshly broken heart, so my fuse is already lit. "Sorry, I'm not a ray of sunshine," I snap.

"Oh, you're a ray of something, that's for sure."

I dump a load of hand towels next to the sheets, not caring that I'm loading the cart all wrong. "You could recite me a poem, or let me know that you're here for me because that's always worked so well." My voice breaks over the way I spew back all the kindness Mina has shown me.

I spin back to the supply rack, but Mina steps in front of me, grabbing my arms, and pinning them to my side. "Nope. No poem today. You can stand there and tell me you're fine, or that you don't care, that you don't need anything from anyone, and that I can't possibly understand. But I am on your side." Mina squeezes tighter, fighting against my unseen torrent of emotions. "I am on your side. Do you understand what that means?" I don't move a muscle. "It means you can throw this hissy fit, and push me away all you want, but I'm not going anywhere. I want to help you. I'll help you restock Hector. I'll help you with your rooms if that's what you need."

I'm shaking from everything that happened yesterday, and from the firm pressure of Mina's love. "I don't need your help!" I shout.

Mina shakes her head but doesn't remove her hands. "I'm not letting go until you tell me something true, because I don't believe you."

I wrench out of her arms and shove Hector so hard that he crashes into an unopened box of paper towels. "I. Don't. Need. Help."

Mina stands her ground, like a river that could carve a

canyon through the earth. "Tell me something true, Rindy." I lean against the locker, trying to control my breathing. My heart is made from granite, but it's starting to crumble. I don't understand why she doesn't walk away from me like everyone else in my life.

She says it again. "Tell me something true."

The truth. I can't keep my heart locked any longer, and my knees buckle. I fall to the floor crying like I did when I understood for the first time that no one was ever going to pick me, not when there were newborns and toddlers for families to choose. Younger kids were more desirable because some adults believe little kids come with less of a past. They just didn't realize that the trauma of being abandoned to the system lives inside your bones no matter how old you are.

I cover my face with my hands, finally allowing myself to cry. "I'm on my own. I've never had anyone." My crying before was a whimper compared to the sobbing that overtakes my body after I finally admit the truth to Mina. She doesn't care that my face is covered in snot and tears, she hugs me like I'm hers, like she'll never let go.

It takes me a long time to stop crying, and when I do I grimace at the mess I've made of Mina's apron. I wipe my hand across my eyes, feeling how swollen they are. "I'm sorry," I say, my chest hurting.

Mina brushes at her soaked shoulder before pulling me to my feet. "It's like yesterday, when I forgot to check the tub's faucet and had a little shower when I turned it on." I can picture her sputtering under a surprise shower, and even in this state it makes me smile.

Mina pulls out her phone, tapping it against her thigh, deciding what to do. Her eyes find mine. "I'm going to make a call, and I need you to wait for me right there," she says.

I don't have the energy to wonder what she's doing. I feel as if I've hiked straight up Big Mountain, so I take a seat on the same box I slammed Hector into. Mina steps outside the room for her call and is back in the room before I've caught my breath.

"I called Syd and Sadie, they're on their way. I'm taking you with me," Mina says.

Sadie and Syd are retired sisters who clean on Tuesday and Wednesday when Mina and I take our weekend. I want to protest, but I don't have the energy. My protests wouldn't get very far with Mina anyway.

We're at the end of the B Hive's driveway now, and I'm wondering where we are going when Mina says, "I'd like you to show me where you've been living." I back up a step, but Mina takes hold of my hand. "Remember, I'm on your side."

Adjusting the straps to my backpack, I consider taking her to the apartment I've had for less than twenty-four hours, swinging open the door, and announcing, "See, everything has been fine. My life is grand." But after everything she's done, and the fact that I covered her shirt in snot, Mina deserves the whole truth.

We trek down the mountain of a hill that the Hive clings to, and wind our way south through town. We keep walking even when the residential houses are a memory behind us. I cut through a path I've worn in the grass to the backside of the dune, arriving at the foundation of a never-built house and the canoe rack I've called home since I arrived in Tinlee Bay.

Mina scuffs her foot across the edge of the foundation as we pass. "I forgot this place was out here. Did you ever hear the story?" I've made up several of my own, but I don't know the truth. Mina says, "Some up-and-comer from the Bay Area decided to build a weekend getaway." She shakes her head. "The story goes they were driving up one weekend and he fell asleep. He survived without a scratch; his wife was killed. He never came back."

I shiver. It's exactly the kind of story I never wanted to let myself imagine. There is always too much tragedy in life. Letting my backpack fall to the ground, I scoot under the canoe. It's strange how normal this is, how familiar it feels, a homecoming in its own right. I won't miss this patch of dirt, but I'm thankful I found it, thankful it sheltered me. I wonder if the wife loved to canoe, and if these vessels belonged to her. Closing my eyes, I imagine her on the inlet in this tiny boat, her face tipped to the sun. I press a finger-nail into the rotting wood right next to the words I scrawled months ago, *home is where the heart is*. When I release my finger a half circle remains. "I'm sorry," I whisper.

I watch Mina's legs step closer, and then she's sitting on the ground. "You're almost invisible under there."

I roll back out, pulling my knees to my chin. "Story of my life."

On the other side of the dunes the ocean slaps against the sand and a breeze pushes through the pine branches above my head. It's always been peaceful here, which is one of the reasons I loved this spot in its own way. It reminded me of Sylvia's porch. And just like the nights I spent on her porch when she'd let me ask her anything I wanted, I tell Mina a story about a gas station and a cardboard box, about parents that never came back for me and a system that tried but never worked.

When I'm done Mina's face is in her hands and her voice is quiet. "No one deserves any of that, Rindy."

"I don't need you to feel sorry for me." I don't mean to sound so defensive, it's an instinct to protect myself and make the truth less painful. Mina blinks at me. It will take time to untangle that habit. I hang my head. "I'm sorry, I don't know how else to react."

Mina tilts my chin until I'm looking at her and not the pile of pine needles I'm collecting next to my shoe. "I am so proud of you," she says, reaching past me, and smacking the side of the canoe. "You found a place to keep yourself safe even when it must have been scary. I am so proud of you. Has anyone ever told you that before?"

I shake my head before burying my face into my knees. Crying must be contagious, like when someone yawns and it spreads down the line. Because there are tears making tracks down Mina's face now. I bite my lip until I taste blood, but start crying anyway.

"You shouldn't be proud of me. I ruin everything." My voice is muffled against my legs.

"We all wear that title from time to time, but maybe things are not as bad as you think," she says.

Without taking my eyes off the ground, and without divulging Lambert family secrets, I tell Mina another story, one about finding friends and losing them.

Mina squeezes my knee. "Look at me." It takes me a long time, but I finally lift my head. "I haven't known you very long, but I've seen you. There's a kind of fire in your bones that nothing in your life can steal from you. I don't know what might happen if you try to talk to Nolan or Lacie, but if you were the one who broke things, you need to be the one to fix them."

I lower my chin back to my knees. "They won't want me to."

Mina stands up, dusting the dirt from her pants. "That could very well be true." She reaches a hand down to me to help me to my feet. "But what if they do?"

27

The buzz of Mina's question stays in my mind for the rest of the day. I take a shower that is hotter and longer than any shower I've ever taken in my life simply because I can. I broke Nolan's trust. I turned Lacie's life upside down. If my past is any sort of teacher about how to live, the lesson I learned over and over again is when relationships break, people trade you in for a newer model. You don't roll up your sleeves and take a risk to fix what is broken.

But what if I tried? What if I could fix my friendship with Lacie?

It would be nice to have her here with me, to help me unpack. Even though moving the four shirts, two pairs of leggings, and my Oh Suds Up muumuu from my backpack to a drawer isn't something I need help with. It's having a friend at my side that I miss. I couldn't fold the dress she made for me into a drawer and it's hanging from the bathroom door. The problem with having all this space to myself is that now I realize how empty it is. Even if I try to fix things with Lacie, and it doesn't go well, at least I tried. Everyone gave up on me in the past, and all I wanted was a second chance.

I flop on the bed. My heart convulses like a fish gasping for air every time I remember the way Nolan kissed me. I have zero knowledge about romantic relationships, but you don't have to be a kiss scholar to know that that kiss meant goodbye. There have been plenty of goodbyes in my life and I don't know how to undo those. Goodbyes are closed doors, and I was never given a key. Lying here thinking about Nolan hurts too much, so I launch myself off the bed and out the door.

The porch light flickers as I walk up the steps of Lacie's house. I don't know how to start a conversation with her, but I need to try. I don't realize I'm clenching my hands into tight balls until I uncurl my fingers to press the doorbell. Part of me wants to walk away and count ringing the doorbell as trying to make amends. Part of me wants to lie down on the porch and wait for Lacie to find me. All of me wishes I was never in this position, to begin with. I should never have told Lacie something that wasn't mine to tell.

When Poh Poh answers the door, she thumps her

walking stick to the floor with a force that makes me jump back. "I was wondering if I could talk to Lacie," I say.

Without a word Poh Poh leaves the door open a crack, retreating into the house only to return a second later. "She doesn't want to see you."

As much as it stings, I'm glad Poh Poh doesn't sugarcoat the message. If I were Lacie, I wouldn't want to see me either. "I'm sorry." I twist the ends of my hair together. "I never should have said anything. I'm really sorry."

Poh Poh stares at me, her lips making a straight line. There's nothing for either of us to say so I turn to go. When my foot reaches their front yard, Poh Poh says, "Sometimes ripping the curtains off the wall to let the light in is the right thing to do." I turn around. "Like a Band-Aid." She makes a motion across her arm as if she were pulling one off her skin. "Fast. Leave a bandage on too long, the wound will never heal." She thumps her cane and goes inside.

I don't feel better about what I did to Lacie, but Poh Poh has succeeded in making me think about the situation in a different way. Of course we want to cover something that hurts, so we can protect it, it's what I've done my entire life— cover the truth so I don't have to see it. But Poh Poh is also right, if we leave a wound covered all the time, it won't heal, it will fester. Mina taught me that. Maybe Lacie just needs time.

I still don't want to be alone in my apartment because all I will notice is how everyone who could fill the space with me is currently not talking to me. But when I arrive at the beach, I don't want to be there either. The sand between my toes isn't a comfort. This is the beach where I met Lacie and Wick and Nolan. It belonged to us, not me. I walk along the promenade, heading south, wondering if I should spend one last night under my canoe when a solitary figure walking across the edge of the seawall makes me stop. Hoping the growing shadows cover me, I turn to go the other way as Wick shouts, "Hey, Rindy, wait."

His flip-flops slap as he runs, and I brace for impact. I really don't want Wick to hate me, but I hurt the people he loves, so it's exactly what I expect. It wouldn't matter if I sprinted away, he'd catch up with me, so I wait where I am. I might as well get this over with and add the last nail to my coffin of ruined friendships.

Wick jogs up to me. "I figured it out this morning. Your inner animal is a deer."

Maybe Wick doesn't know what happened. Is it possible he hasn't seen Lacie or Nolan? I try to calm my racing heart, pretending this isn't my last normal conversation with him before he realizes what I did. "Why a deer?" I ask.

"They have good instincts, like they trust their gut, you know, but they are always a little skittish, on edge. Afraid. Sniffing the air for danger." I take in what he's telling me and when he puts his hand on my shoulder, I know what he's going to say next. "Lacie told me what happened." His voice drops to a whisper. "Also, I didn't see that coming. Calvin is her dad." Wick shakes his head and whistles.

It's a strange comfort that he knows the truth. But

confusing because he saw me, and he could have avoided me like I wanted to do. Or he could have run up to me and shouted in my face. Instead, he is Wick as usual.

"Lacie doesn't want to see me," I say and Wick nods. What have his conversations with Lacie been like? I attempt to be lighthearted even though it's the last thing I feel, but somehow it's what Wick brings out in everyone around him. "She can't stay mad forever, right?"

He tips his head from side to side and winces. "She's more hurt than mad," he says.

Picturing Lacie curled up on her bed hurting from a wound I caused is worse than knowing she's in her room throwing darts at an image of my face.

Wick tips his head up the promenade the way I came. "I made you something," he says.

At an unmarked door, Wick pulls a key from his pocket and unlocks it. Flicking on the light reveals that we are standing in a warehouse where every last inch is covered with stacked cardboard boxes, their lids flopped or ripped open. Walking past one, I see piles of T-shirts in every color imaginable.

"This is Stacia's place." My mind rolls through the list of his sisters. Stacia, the one who owns a print shop. Wick reaches to the top of a shelf and pulls something down. It's a folded piece of fabric. "Lamby left early in the morning," Wick says.

I pitch forward, trying to catch my breath from the punch of Wick's words. Nolan is gone. Wick reaches out an arm to steady me, handing me what he grabbed from the shelf above his head. Lacie doesn't want to talk to me, and now there is no way I can fix what happened with Nolan. He said his goodbye and there was nothing left for him to do but leave.

Wick unfolds a shirt, holding it in front of him. Black typewriter words are printed on the white shirt. *My boyfriend went to the Pando and all I got was this shirt.* The words swirl together in my tear-filled vision.

Wick punches my arm. "Too soon?"

Something like a croak erupts from my mouth. "He's not my boyfriend."

Wick shrugs. "I don't know, there's something about the two of you. If it were legal for me to place bets, I'd bet on Team NonDairy." I raise an eyebrow. "What? Don't look at me like that. You try making a team out of the letters from your names. Rinoland? No." He shakes his head. "NonDairy is a solid option."

Laughing while crying creates the worst case of hiccups, making my chest hurt. "Why are you doing this? Why are you nice to me when I hurt your best friends? It would make more sense if you hated me too."

"Nobody hates you." Wick hugs me. "Do you know how many times I do something I regret? At least once a day." He releases me and I love how he owns his own chaos. "Anyway. I haven't eaten in like three minutes and I'm starving. You don't think going for ice cream would be against the rules, even if we are Team NonDairy, do you?"

It's my turn to hug him. "What do people do without a Wick in their life?" I ask.

"Make questionable choices." You could land an airplane on the wide swath of Wick's smile. "But then again, having a Wick in your life gets you the exact same results." He locks the door to his sister's shop. "I'm going to have double fudge ripple. What about you? Ooh, wait, let me guess." He closes his eyes and holds his hand to my forehead as if he's a mind reader or trying to detect a fever.

He's ridiculous and right now he's the only friend I have. "Thank you, Wick."

"Don't thank me yet, I haven't guessed your favorite flavor." He takes another moment, his forehead creased in concentration. "You, my friend, are in need of cookies and cream."

I smack his arm. "How did you know?" There are several flavors I'd pick before cookies and cream, but I'm not going to tell Wick that. In fact, from now on it is going to be my favorite because it will always remind me of how to be a friend.

28

Mina told me I didn't have to come in today, but I refused her offer. There is no way I could spend the day alone in my apartment. When I get to Hector, another summons to Beverly's office is waiting for me. It's written on the same square stationary that was attached to my bonus, and this one doesn't come with a smiley face after her name. Or a free breakfast.

I can't find Mina. I could use a little reinforcement before I face Beverly. By now she obviously knows her son left, and I have some explaining to do about how I dropped my end of the bargain. Not that I ever agreed to her unwritten request but then again, I did cash the check.

I've stalled as long as I can by searching each floor for Mina with no success. But when Beverly opens her door, I finally find her.

"We were just talking about you," Beverly says.

What have they been discussing? Did Mina tell Beverly everything I shared with her yesterday?

One spring break, my case worker signed me up for a camp at the YMCA. There was a sauna in the locker room we were not allowed to use, but I didn't want to play dodgeball in the gym with everyone else, so I sat in the wooden box until it was too hard to breathe. When I finally pushed myself out the door, I collapsed on the cold tiles next to the lockers.

That same hot, about-to-pass-out feeling clings to my skin. "I already spent the bonus," I say. "There's no way I can pay you back. Not right now anyway, but I could. I will."

Beverly is holding the door open for me to walk through. "Why don't you come in first," she says.

I'm still lightheaded as I take a seat next to Mina, and Beverly maneuvers behind her desk. My leg bounces up and down, and even though Mina rests her hand on my thigh, I can't keep my mouth shut. "I lied in my interview. I have no idea if Rindy is an old family name. I never met my parents." My eyes once again flick to the gigantic family portrait on the wall behind Beverly, but it doesn't seem as perfect as it did the first time I saw it. Nothing ever does. Neither Beverly nor Mina have said a word and I can't stop talking. "Also. I'm the one who told Lacie the truth. I'm sorry."

Smoothing my hands down my smock, I take a deep breath and feel surprisingly calm after everything I vomited out of my mouth. There are no more lies for me to hide behind.

Beverly tucks a strand of hair behind her ear. "Anything else you'd like to add?" she asks.

I shake my head. "No. I'm good."

Beverly smiles at Mina and for the first time, her face doesn't seem pinched or fake. "She reminds me of you when we first—"

"I'm telling you, there's a fire in her," Mina interrupts.

"I believe there is. A fire my son certainly noticed, but we'll get to that in a moment. First, I need to apologize."

My head jerks back in surprise. Beverly wanted me to convince Nolan to stay, but he already left, and I just admitted that I was the one who told Lacie who her father is, and now Beverly is going to tell me sorry?

"You don't need to pay back anything. That was a low move of me to make, something I remembered from one of Calvin's many stories. I never should have put you in that position. Will you forgive me?"

I nod, not trusting my voice.

Beverly clasps her hands on top of her desk, letting out a sigh. "The truth was bound to come out sooner or later. I can't say it's easy, but keeping it hidden took its own toll." Pressing her hands to the surface of her desk, Beverly stands, signaling that is all she's going to say about Lacie and her husband. She walks around to the front of her desk, leaning on the edge in front of me. "Now, about my idiot son." For the second time in less than a minute, my head jerks back in surprise as Beverly keeps talking. "All a mother ever wants is for their baby to be healthy and happy. Somehow, it's easy to lose sight of that over the years. Or think I know what's best. I have never seen him happier than he was this summer, and based on what I saw at the gala, I'm guessing the same goes for you." She leans forward. "He told me he asked you to go with him, so here's my proposition."

When Beverly is done talking my head is spinning. Nolan is in Arches National Park and Beverly offered to drive me there. If he doesn't want me anywhere near him, we'll come straight home, and she'll still pay me for the days I missed.

I don't have to risk anything. Except for everything.

Nolan could take one look at me and say no thanks, I'd rather not trust you again. He might refuse to see me, the same way Lacie did.

"Take as much time as you need to decide," Beverly says.

There is nothing for me to consider. Nolan is so young in the family photo that hangs on the wall. His entire life was stretching out in front of him, waiting for him to discover it. When I was his age, I was waiting too and now Beverly is giving me a chance to go to him, see him face-to-face, and explain my heart. It might not go well, but I'll feel better for trying instead of letting Nolan leave without knowing the truth.

Nervous energy pushes me out of my chair. Seeing Nolan again is a wildfire rush of desire across my skin. "I accept your offer, on one condition." Beverly lifts a questioning eyebrow. "Mina comes with."

At that, Mina slaps her knee. "Road trip!"

29

So much for unpacking. Everything I own is once again stuffed inside my backpack, and I can't help but wonder if I am making a giant mistake. I toss the backpack on the couch, reminding myself that no matter what happens, I'm not giving up a place to live. If Nolan never wants to see me again, I still have an apartment and a job. Trusting Mina and Beverly with the truth has given me a safety net I never expected, and accepting a ride to Utah is an offer I can't refuse, even if I'm afraid.

But between wondering what Nolan's reaction will be, and waiting for the early morning wake-up I know is coming, I can't sleep. So, when Beverly finally knocks on my door, I fling it open because I've been standing there waiting. She's wearing denim shorts with a Red Sox T-shirt half tucked in, half not, with sunglasses on her head like a headband. I must be having a sleep-deprived hallucination. Mina stands next to her in a similar fashion holding out a paper cup of coffee. "Every good adventure starts at an unreasonable hour," Mina says.

They seem far too awake at four in the morning, and no doubt it has something to do with the caffeine. I gladly accept the coffee and take a last glance over my shoulder. What if Nolan still wants me to go with him? What would it be like to have him as my home instead of these four walls? Am I ready to agree to that and leave the security of this newfound apartment behind? Pulling the door closed, I tuck the key in my pocket, knowing full well I might be staggering back through this door two days from now holding my broken heart in my hands.

Beverly and Mina wait for me to step away from the door, standing next to the Lexus I saw parked in the garage when Nolan took me on the motorcycle, the day he first kissed me. That was a perfect afternoon. Would Nolan like to have more afternoons like that? The only way to find out is to get into Beverly's car. I know I'm not turning my back on a place to live, but it feels like I am.

Going on a road trip with Beverly and Mina is not something I ever pictured happening. I should be used to that fact since pretty much nothing in my life is how I pictured it. Some of it has been for the worse, and some for the better. Finding Nolan, Wick, and Lacie was definitely on the better end but even that didn't go so well. Leaving things unresolved with Lacie is painful, but at least I tried.

Watching Mina and Beverly be best friends helps pass

the time, and keeps my mind off the seek-and-find mission we're on. They're complete opposites in every possible way. Mina wants music, and Beverly prefers talk radio. Beverly refuses to pull over at rest stops, insisting they are unsanitary, and neither of us can argue with that. As we get closer to Reno, Mina wins the radio battle and cranks a Whitney Houston love song. She whips around to me, her fist becoming a microphone as she belts the lyrics.

My face is on fire as she sings. How am I supposed to react to this when Nolan's mom is driving the car? Trying to ignore the fact that Nolan is the boy I dream about is pointless, it's the whole reason the three of us are in this car in the first place. But I avoid looking at Beverly because even though we all know it's true, it's still awkward.

Despite my burning cheeks, I clap when it's over. "You can really sing," I say.

"You should see her at Strike the High Note when she hosts karaoke night," Beverly says and Mina catches my eye.

We remember the same afternoon when she slid into the booth Nolan and I shared. It was the day Mina found out I'd been lying to everyone, and the weight of that memory is so uncomfortable I squirm under my seatbelt. It's not only that I betrayed Nolan's trust when I told Lacie who her father was, it's that I've never been completely honest with him in the first place. He doesn't even know my full name.

This trip is a waste of time. We've been driving the better part of the day, and I slump against the leather seat. "We should go home," I say.

"What?" Mina and Beverly say in unison.

I wrap and unwrap a strand of hair around my finger. I'm trying to stop fidgeting with it when I'm nervous but can't seem to stop. "All I've ever done is lie to everyone, and when I explain everything to Nolan he won't want me. No one ever has; why should he be the first?"

Beverly drums her fingers on the steering wheel. "I know what we need." She flicks her turn signal on and we take the first exit we've passed in a while. Mina and I are stretching our legs against the tire when Beverly emerges from the gas station, her arms filled with individually wrapped packages that she dumps through the rear window next to my seat. "We needed snacks," she says, reaching back through the window and grabbing a pack of Corn Nuts.

My eyes pop open. Beverly, who only serves organic everything at the B Hive, rips open the packet and dumps some straight into her mouth. "I can't believe you eat that," I say.

She crunches for a while then says, "They are addicting, what are you going to do?" I guess she's human after all. She tosses the keys to Mina. "Your turn."

As Mina walks around the car, Beverly rests her hand on my shoulder. "It's okay to be scared, but I know Nolan." Which is her way of telling me that I shouldn't be afraid, but it's too late for that.

It's well past ten o'clock when we turn into the Devil's Garden Campground, and the headlights stab the night air in front of us as we slowly wind along the main road. With a name this inviting, what can possibly go wrong? Nolan is somewhere in this long stretch of campsites, and I'm about to find him. *It's okay to be scared. It's okay to be scared.* But my heart doesn't believe the words. Leaning forward, I rest my chin on the back of Beverly's seat as she taps open an app to find Nolan's location. The map slides across the screen as a pin with his face drops in place. Nolan is so close. I roll my window down because I need a breeze on my face. All I get is arid air that seems brittle enough to snap in half. I close my eyes, taking deep breaths as the car slows. What am I supposed to say when I see him?

Mina pulls to the shoulder and turns off the engine. This is it. I've twisted my hair into a knot I cannot untangle. So much for breaking the habit.

They turn to look at me. "We'll wait here," Beverly offers.

I'm not ready to be alone and face whatever is about to happen. I know Nolan won't hurt me, not on purpose. If anyone is about to hurt anyone, it will probably be my fault, all over again. "Could you both walk with me?" I don't want to admit that underneath all my other fears, there's still a deep river of unease that they will drive away, leaving me stranded.

They are out their doors faster than I am, walking in front of me like a shield. My legs shake the closer we get. This is Nolan, and I know him too—he is kind, and somehow, he loves me; at least he used to. I don't know what a panic attack feels like but the pressure in my chest makes it hard for me to take a breath. The soft orange glow of a fire is a welcome mat, but my feet drag in the dirt. This is like the first night I walked the beach in Tinlee Bay; the night I met Nolan and Lacie and Wick at his birthday bonfire. Except, this time as I approach the flames I'm not alone, I have Beverly and Mina with me. I take a deep breath. I'm ready to see Nolan again.

As I round the boulder sticking out of the red dirt, I discover Nolan isn't alone.

30

There are several people around the fire, but the familiar slope of Nolan's shoulder is easy to find in the shadows thrown by the flames. It's currently occupied by a girl with shimmering blond hair, so shiny it reflects the moonlight. I should have known this was what I would find. We didn't need to drive an entire day to discover what I've always known. I am easily replaceable. I've never been the sort of person who gets a happily ever after. At least not like this. Not with someone like Nolan. Guys like Nolan attract girls like the one next to him, girls who are still wearing a bikini top with short shorts, even though the sun is long gone. She must be freezing.

My hand flies to my mouth, but a whimper slides past my finger. Nolan turns at the strange sound, jumping from the log. My instinct is to run, to get as far away as possible, to protect what's left of my heart. But Mina puts her hand on my back, reminding me she is with me and stopping me from running in the other direction.

Nolan's mom stands next to me and he has known Mina his entire life. But it's my name that Nolan says. "Rindy." His voice is laced with the same barbwire cut of emotion as when he kissed me goodbye. It's an earthquake that tilts the axis of my heart.

When Sylvia told me there was a stretch of trail where she could feel the rotation of the earth, and she knew she was home, I started chasing that idea, wanting to find the place where I belong. I've been desperate to find my own latitude and longitude, the place where my heart skipped a beat, the place where I knew I was home.

Turns out, it's not a trail, a beach, a mountain, or an apartment, that my heart has been searching for. It's him. It's Nolan.

The earth keeps tilting beneath my feet as he walks closer. "What are you doing here?" he asks. No smile. No hug.

Mina squeezes my hand, but it doesn't give me enough strength to say anything. The group of people behind Nolan have swiveled their heads to watch whatever is about to unfold.

I never should have come. Beverly steps toward the strangers sitting around the fire. Watching her talk to them feels like having the TV muted. I have no idea what she said, but a moment later they march in line down a path back to wherever they belong.

Beverly rests her hand on Nolan's shoulder and he blinks at her as if he's just woken up and has no idea where he is. She doesn't offer any explanation for our unannounced arrival. "We'll wait at the car," she tells us.

Mina gives my hand another squeeze, and then I'm alone with Nolan. I reach for the ends of my hair but it's a knot at my shoulder. There's nothing for my hands to do so I shove them in my pockets. Then pull them out again, grasping them behind my back.

"My parents and I were never having a screen free summer." This is not anywhere close to the sentences I rehearsed as we drove, but it's as good of a place as any to start. "In order for that to happen, I'd have to have parents." My heart is racing because there's so much to explain and I don't know how to find all the words I need. "I aged out of the foster system, and I've been sleeping under a canoe rack since I got to Tinlee Bay. I wasn't on vacation."

Nolan rubs his hand across his chin, but he doesn't say anything. I can't stand the silence. This feels too much like all the other goodbyes I've lived through. One day my life has to make sense, but it's not going to be today.

There's still so much Nolan doesn't know.

"I wasn't staying at the B Hive," I say, grabbing the knot of hair, and prying it apart with my fingers, not caring that it hurts. "I got a job there cleaning rooms. That's how I know Mina."

Nolan kicks at the dirt with the toe of his boot. Why

won't he look at me? I want him to say something, but he hasn't.

He finally lifts his head. "Was everything a lie?"

It's almost as if Nolan has knocked me over. I wish he'd go back to kicking the dirt with his shoe. My fingers rip through a knot and a tear slides out the corner of my eye. "Not the important parts."

Nolan nods and takes a deep breath. "You could have trusted me."

I could have done a lot of things, but I didn't.

I want to grab Nolan's hand, to feel the warmth of his skin, so I can hold on tight and stop feeling like I'm about to fade into the air, but my fingers are still stuck in the twists of hair. More tears slide down my face. Why won't Nolan reach for me?

"I did trust you," I say.

Nolan kicks the same patch of dirt as before. His eyes dart to the ground and then back to mine. "Not enough."

31

Not enough.

Of all the things Nolan ever said to me, this is the truest one. I am not enough. I never have been, or somebody would have let me stay.

Nolan keeps kicking the dirt, but it might as well be my heart. He huffs out a breath. "I'll go get Mom and Mina," he says, walking past me.

I don't know how long Nolan is gone because I don't move. I'm still breathing even though it doesn't feel like I am because I'm still standing. Mina puts her arm around my shoulder and says, "It's too late to do anything else, so we're all going to stay the night here." She gives my arm a squeeze. "Nolan says there's room in the tent for the three of us."

I shake my head. "I'm fine out here."

Nolan is adding a log to the fire, his back is to me, and it tenses right before the plume of embers scatters across the night. He stands, climbs the ladder, and returns with a sleeping bag that he hands to me before he walks to the other side of the campsite.

Mina tries to convince me to come into the tent, but gives up, leaving me outside hugging the sleeping bag to my chest. It smells like Nolan and I bury my face in it. I'm shivering, not only from the chill in the air, but from everything in my life that I've ruined.

There is not a great place to rest. Nolan is on the one side of his 4Runner, so I claim the other. There is no felled tree or rock or berm of dirt to lean against or offer protection. I'm alone and exposed. It is not what could be hidden in the shadows lurking behind me that scares me and will not let me sleep, it's what's in front of me, on the other side of the car. It's Nolan. He's sitting next to the fire, poking it with a stick, causing the logs to crackle and fall.

Is he remembering the way our hands fit together the same way I am?

I close my eyes, forcing myself to go back in time to Wick's bonfire. The sand beneath my feet was a new sensation and the straps of my backpack dug into my shoulders. The rise and fall of easy conversation floating around the flames had been a comfort. Lacie smiled as Wick rested his chin on her shoulder and Nolan sat in the shadows. If only I knew I could trust them with my battered heart. How could I have known these people were different from everyone I ever met before?

I didn't know, and now I've destroyed the safest place my heart ever had.

The morning light is thin when I get up and walk to the crest of a hill. In the distance are curious shadows that I assume are rock formations. I'm a million miles away from any geography I could call home. Today I'll shove my backpack in the trunk of Beverly's car, and we'll make the long drive back to Tinlee Bay. At least this time I have an apartment and a job. It's more than I had when I first arrived.

"Would you rather spend a week alone in the forest, or a night alone in a haunted house?"

Nolan's raspy voice startles me and I make a sound in my throat, my hand flying to my chest. He's standing next to me, his eyes fixed on the landscape pockmarked with shadows. This is the same question that made me blurt my answer at the bonfire. This time my answer is nothing more than a whisper, but it's still the same. It will always be the same answer.

"Forest," I say.

My pulse beats a rhythm against my ribs and Nolan takes a shaky breath. "That's the first thing I ever knew about you and that wasn't a lie." Nolan touches my elbow before stepping in front of me. "Why didn't you tell me?" His face is creased with more questions.

Nolan is close enough that I can smell the campfire clinging to his skin and I want to press my face in the soft spot next to his shoulder, but I can't.

"I didn't know how." I pull apart another knot in my hair,

tears stinging the corners of my eyes before I even start. "I was afraid. No one ever—" My voice catches. "No one ever made room for me or showed me I could trust them. Not until yo—" I can't finish. A tidal wave of emotions crashes over my heart and it's not the ripping out of hair that is making me cry, it's ripping the truth out of my heart and letting Nolan see how alone and scared I am that makes me sob. I'm still not sure Nolan wants anything to do with me.

Nolan reaches for my hand, clasping his around the fingers still grasping the ends of my hair.

"How come you never told Lacie the truth?" I blurt the question, and his hand falls to his side. I take a step back because I'm still ruining my life. "I'm sorry, it's none of my business."

He pushes his hand through his hair before finding mine again. "Maybe not. But we've both kept the truth hidden from people." He takes a breath. "I think we did it for the same reasons. You were protecting yourself."

It had to have been a shock for Nolan to discover Lacie is his half-sister but not as big of a shock as finding out his dad had an affair. He said we did what we did for the same reason, and he was right about my reason. "You were protecting your mom?"

It was a guess, but Nolan nods. After everything I've done, he might never be the king of my hand-selected tribe, but Nolan is a good man. He will always protect the people he loves.

"Did you ever know her?" he asks.

It takes me a moment to understand the leap in our conversation. I mentioned his mom, and now he's asking me about mine. I start to back up again; I don't like staring these facts in the face, but Nolan is holding my hand, and he won't let me back away. "No." My throat is so tight, it feels as if there is no more air to breathe. "My name is Rindy Jane Doe because someone found me in a box at a gas station and no one ever came back to claim me." I clear my throat with a cough, so I won't start to cry.

"You never had anyone show you how to trust them." He wraps his arms around me. His touch doesn't make the truth go away, but it is a comfort. "I could have helped you."

I nod my head against his shoulder, my lips trembling. "I needed to do it on my own."

He steps out of our embrace. "I have to do this on my own too." He spreads his arms out as if they are big enough to encircle the beautiful vista behind him. "I have to figure out who I am away from the shadow of my dad."

My knees almost give out, but somehow, I'm still standing. This is it; this is where I'll say goodbye to Nolan. I can't even be mad that he wants to figure his life out on his own, because I understand. I had the same jackhammer of desire pounding my heart every day. I had my chance with Nolan, and I lost it.

I was right, I'll never be enough.

But then he takes a step toward me. "I need to figure out who I am away from my dad, but that doesn't mean I don't want you. If I asked you to stay with me, what would you say?"

The sun emerges above the desert, and the red earth glows as if it's enchanted with magic. There's no familiar forest to hem me in, or waves to pull me out. There is only Nolan and the same question he asked before he left.

I bite my lip so hard it almost bleeds. I'm not sure I'll ever get used to letting what's trapped inside my heart be heard. "I'd say I'm scared. Part of me will always be afraid." I find his other hand and intertwine my fingers with his. "But I'd also say you are the only person who has ever made me feel like I am home."

Nolan pulls me into his arms, and like cotton candy I dissolve when his lips find mine. I am still nowhere close to being a kiss scholar, but this kiss is not hello or goodbye. This kiss is a promise.

After breakfast, we made a two-car convoy to Salt Lake City. Mina and Beverly follow behind me and Nolan. He keeps reaching over to grab my hand as if he can't believe I'm with him, and I hold tight because I can't quite believe it either. I might not have a house with four walls around me, but Nolan is offering me the four chambers of his heart. It's more than I ever dared dream of.

When we get to the city we drive straight to the mall. Beverly links her arm through Nolan's. "I need some time with my son. We'll meet back here in say, three hours?" Beverly asks.

I don't want to let Nolan out of my sight, but Beverly is his mom, and she can ask for whatever she wants. Mina mirrors Beverly's motion and links her arm through mine. "See ya then," Mina says.

Nolan follows wherever Beverly and he are headed, but I don't have time to wonder if he knows where they are going because Mina gives my arm a little squeeze. "All right. Three hours. What do you need?" she asks.

I cock my head to the side. "I don't need anything," I say, and Mina gives me a face that I can only describe as *Yeah right* and asks again. This is Mina, she's as safe of a place as they come, and she won't laugh at me. "I could use some new underwear," I admit.

Mina buys me more than a new pack of underwear. I now have a duffel bag full of shirts and shorts, new leggings, a pair of pajamas, and after she saw me staring at the rack for a very long time, a swimsuit. It's not kelly green, or a bikini, but it's mine and that's all that matters.

"Mina, this is too much." It's hard for me to accept focused attention on fulfilling my basic needs.

She shakes her head, sending her curls bouncing. "Nonsense." She takes out her phone to check the time. "One more stop, let's go."

I don't know where we are headed until we set foot in the cell phone store. The walls glow a neon pink and so does our skin. She walks straight to the bored teenager behind the counter. "I need to add her to my plan," Mina says.

I grab her arm. "Mina, no, this is too much, I can't let you do this."

Her hand is firm on the counter. "Having a phone is non-negotiable." She turns back to the sales attendant, talking to him, not me. It takes longer than we anticipated, but when it's all done, the employee hands me back my phone, which has now been reactivated and added to Mina's plan.

I still have some money in my account, but not much, and it won't last long. "Can I at least pay you something?" I ask.

"Eventually, but not anytime soon." Mina stops at the threshold of the store. "Seems to me you need some time in your life where you don't have to worry about anything, and I'm more than happy to make that happen for you."

I used to imagine what my mom would be like. The mom I conjured up was mean and impractical, the sort of person who snapped at me for no reason and wore kitten heels in eight inches of fresh snow. The pretend mom that lived inside my head was cynical because she had to be. I couldn't imagine her any other way. It hurt too much if I tried to pretend she was compassionate. If I ever would've allowed myself to create a mom who loved me, she would be exactly like Mina. I throw my arms around her.

Beverly booked us into a hotel for the night. Two rooms. One for Mina, myself, and her. One for Nolan. "I'm still your mother after all," she tells him, handing him his own keycard as his face turns into a flame. Then she takes us to dinner at the restaurant.

The buffet is a sight to behold; it's almost too much food to look at. Wick's voice inside my head tells me there could never be too much food. I hope somewhere, in all of this, there will be cookies and cream. "I wish Wick could see this," I say.

We each grab a plate. "He'd probably make himself sick," Nolan laughs.

I clench the plate to my chest. "He would, then he'd lie on the floor, moaning for Lacie to take care of him." The smile on my face hurts, but not as much as I hurt Lacie.

I don't want to leave my friendship with Lacie in this shattered state, but I don't know when I'll see her again. Beverly and Mina are already ahead of us filling their plates. Maybe Lacie shut Nolan out too? Which is a strange thing to wish for.

"Have you heard from Lacie?" I ask.

Nolan nods. "She texted me late last night, which reminds me." He digs his phone out of his pocket. "This is for you."

I'm still squeezing the plate to my chest when Nolan hands me his phone. The text message is already open, and inside the blue bubble, it says, *Have Rindy call me.*

Lacie wants to talk to me. My mind swirls with possibilities. It could be good, or maybe she wants to yell at me. Maybe I don't want to talk to Lacie after all.

Nolan watches me, my face scrunched, holding a plate like a life raft and I'm drowning, so I tell him what happened when I went to see her.

He takes the plate out of my hand. "I'll wait."

The phone rings and my stomach flips. "Hey," she answers, clearly thinking it's Nolan.

My mouth has gone dry and my voice cracks. "Lacie, it's me."

The silence is a runaway train. Maybe she changed her mind and doesn't want to talk anymore. But when she starts, I can hardly untangle what she is saying because she's talking so fast. She says, *"I blamed you"* and then it's quiet again. I'm still miles away from knowing how to be vulnerable but I apologize for what I did. Lacie sniffs like she's trying not to cry, and then says she'll call again soon. It was short and I'm not sure anything is healed, but it's a start.

I give Nolan his phone and he hands me back my plate. "Ready?" he asks.

My small smile is the only answer he gets.

All my life I wanted to be surrounded by a family, the bigger the better, and somehow, I ended up making my own.

While I was trying not to be seen, so I could protect my heart, I managed to find people who are willing to do the hard work of sticking around. I know Nolan isn't just asking if I'm ready to go eat, he's making sure I'm okay to keep moving forward. I love him even more for understanding me. For once in my life, I am ready for whatever happens next.

32

Nolan and I are surrounded by bone-white tree trunks scarred with black notches. "Can you believe this?" he whispers under the cathedral of leaves.

I squeeze his hand, unable to find the words I need. It's not the fact that all the trees inside the Pando look the same, it's the fact that they are all the same tree, that I cannot wrap my head around. It's like staring at the reflection of your reflection in a mirror and having it stretch out in a never-ending repetition of your face.

We are standing inside infinity.

There is no one else around. It's only Nolan and I, the trees, and the wind tossing golden leaves.

Tipping my head skyward, I'm dizzy from the tangled view of branches reaching to the brilliant blue sky. White. Black. Blue. Gold. It's a swirl of perfection and I lie on the ground, tugging Nolan down with me. I want to soak in this view as long as possible.

The sky shifts as a few clouds float past, both of us mesmerized by the mass of shivering leaves that dance like a well-rehearsed ballet. If we lay here long enough the leaves would cover us in nature's finest blanket.

Nolan breaks the silence. "Do you remember that guy in Arkansas I told you about?"

The wind dislodges a leaf from its branch and it rides the current like a kite. "The one who can identify a tree by tasting its sawdust?" I ask.

"Yeah. His name is Jay and he's a legend. We've been messaging and he invited us to come out and stay on his property. He's building and refurbishing furniture, and offered me something like an apprenticeship. It could be good for me. And he has goats."

Laughing, I roll onto my side, taking in this view as well. Nolan's eyes are more brilliant than the sky and I brush the hair off his forehead. "Are the goats supposed to sell me on the idea?"

"They are cute. I've seen pictures." Nolan smiles. It's a flash of lightning across his face, and it still levels me every time.

I press my lips to his. "You're cute. I've seen pictures," I say.

It's been a month since we parted ways with Mina and Beverly in Salt Lake, and Nolan has been busy taking pictures wherever we go. Pictures of the trees, our view, our campsite, and more selfies of us than I can count. He says one day we'll print them out and line our walls with these memories. And every time he says that his words sink deeper into my heart. I'm starting to let myself believe in a future with him. He finds ways every day to tell me that he's not going anywhere.

I'm still learning how to trust, and I'm not ready for our relationship to advance past what it is right now, so we take turns with one of us sleeping in the tent and one of us in the hammock outside. Sometimes I wake up in the middle of the night afraid I'll find Nolan gone, so I unzip the flap and shine a flashlight to where I find him sound asleep. He's never mad when that happens. He never pretends that my fear isn't real. He just gets up, stokes the fire, and lets me sit on the ground next to him and the flames until I finally fall asleep again.

Nolan kisses me back now. "So, that's a yes?"

I roll on my back again. I've come a long way since I was abandoned at the gas station. It's never been easy, and there are years I wish I could obliterate or not claim as my story, but I'm here and Nolan squeezes my hand waiting for an answer. "That's a yes," I say.

After a while, we get up and walk even deeper into the maze of trees. It would be easy to lose your bearing without any anchors or markings to tell where you are. The farther into the clone we go, the quieter it is, and the closer the trees grow to each other. The wind barely moves their branches. When I stoop towards the ground, Nolan lets go of my hand, knowing what I'm doing. I gently scuff the fallen leaves with my foot before moving on to a different section, hunting for a perfect leaf. This is my own collection. Every day I find a leaf and press it into the journal Nolan bought me, labeling where I found it. I take a few steps from Nolan and bend down, plucking a golden aspen leaf off the ground. It was all by itself, like it was waiting to be discovered. I had to wait a long time for that to happen to me, but I'm glad someone finally saw me and picked me up too.

A few days ago, Nolan asked if I wanted to go back to Montana so I could show him where I grew up, but I said no. There is nothing for me there. It's where I was found, but it was never home. Maybe one day I'll want to play tour guide for him, but I'm not ready for the fresh sting that driving down those roads would bring, even if Nolan held my hand the whole time.

I twirl the stem between my fingers, holding it out for Nolan to see.

"It looks like a heart," he says.

Nolan waits as I remove my journal from my backpack, pressing the leaf to a page, and jotting a note beside it. Then he gently cups my face in his hands, kissing me under the watchful eye of the forest. The sun drips through the leaves, scattering golden light as it slowly makes its descent for the day. We turn to leave.

As we clear the last row of trees, Nolan and I take one final look at the Pando. He pulls me into the crook of his shoulder and the clouds glow as bright as the quivering leaves.

"We'll come back. Every year," he says.

More promises of a future that I collect inside my heart. "A Pandoversary."

Nolan presses his face into my neck. "You're as bad as Wick sometimes."

I shove him away, but he pulls me right back into his arms, which is the only place I ever want to be.

We already decided that no matter what happens, or where we are, we'll go back to Tinlee Bay for Christmas. Nolan doesn't call Tinlee Bay home anymore. I'm not sure if he does that for my benefit or if it simply stopped being his anchor.

I used to want home to be a lot of things; four walls, my own room, a place I could leave my socks on the floor and no one would yell at me. And as nice as those things are, I finally discovered that home is the hand I hold—not a fixed structure. My home is the wild open space between my heart and Nolan's where our love is a living, breathing thing.

33

My cheeks are chapped from the wind but my hands are full, so I can't pull my scarf over my face. "Hold still, you're making this harder than it needs to be," I say.

Normally Marionberry dips her head like a good little goat so I can slip the sweater down her neck, but not today. Today, she rears on her back legs tipping her head to the side, and before I can get out of her way, she slams her forehead into my hip. It throws me off-balance, and I land with a thud on the ground.

"Need a hand?" Nolan asks, coughing to hide his laughter from escaping.

I stand, dusting the dirt from my jeans. "Nope, I'm good." I throw a smile at him, then fold the sweater I was going to put on Marionberry over my arm, squinting in her direction, but she's already munching on a pile of hay in the corner of the pen. "Someone is going to have to be cold."

"You know she doesn't *need* the sweater, right?" Nolan unlatches the gate, holding it open, his lip curled to one side.

This is a conversation we've had several times, and he's not waiting for a response. Of course, I know a goat doesn't need to wear a sweater. But maybe I need it. Maybe I'm the one who needs to find sweaters at the secondhand store in Jasper and put them on the goats. Especially Marionberry, because who knew you could have a favorite goat and you'd want to make sure she was more than okay.

The gate clicks behind me, and Nolan breathes into his hands before rubbing them together. "Do you want to go for a walk?"

My answer is tossing the sweater onto a nearby log and slipping my hand in his. Nolan squeezes it and begins leading the way deeper into the forest behind Jay's house. The first day of winter is tomorrow, and all the branches are barren. You might think the forest would feel lonesome like this, but it doesn't. It's like reading the sequel to a book you love, familiar but different.

We haven't had any snow yet, and I hope we're back in time for the first flakes to land but I'm not so sure. We leave in the morning to drive to Tinlee Bay for Christmas. My stomach clenches. What will it be like to go back? I've never returned to a place that used to be mine. Granted, the only thing I had in Tinlee Bay was a canoe rack, and I won't be sleeping there. I'm staying with Mina and I can't wait. We talk every week, and I love her more than I did before. Hopefully Christmas dinner with Beverly's famous roasted duck won't be a disaster. I've never eaten duck and I'm not sure I want to start now, but it's a Lambert tradition and I get to be a part of it.

None of that is why my stomach hurts.

Lacie and I messaged a few times after I called her from Salt Lake, but then something happened and she stopped. With my free hand, I trace the rectangle of my phone in my pocket. There are a lot of messages she hasn't replied to. Nolan tells me not to worry. He says it's fine, she's busy, and I believe him. But there's a chance my face is back on a dartboard in her room. It's my fault Lacie's life got turned inside out with the truth.

I walk faster, but Nolan slows me with a gentle tug on my hand. "Where exactly are you taking me?"

Nolan nudges his elbow into my side. "Almost there."

It isn't an answer but I let it be, and we hike the rest of the way with the crunch of our boots and an occasional song of a white-throated sparrow filling the chilly air.

Then Nolan stops. "Okay, I need you to close your eyes now."

"What?" The blue of Nolan's eyes flash, but there's something else, something deeper. Is he nervous? I cock my head to the side. "If I sprain my ankle out here—"

"You won't. Trust me."

I do, more each day, so it's an easy request. "Alright then," I say, closing my eyes, reaching a hand out for Nolan to take so he can guide me the rest of the way. It is slow going but Nolan never lets me trip, and then we finally come to another stop.

"Now before you open your eyes," Nolan says, but he stops and exhales. "I made this for you"—another exhale—"Go ahead, open your eyes."

All that is in front of me is the forest crowded with slumbering trees, and I reach for my hair but stop myself from relying on my nervous habit. Nolan is silent next to me, his gaze settled on something farther past the rows of trees closest to us. And there, perched on a branch is a tree house resembling a birdhouse with an A-frame roof and a circular window above the door. It has a tiny wraparound porch and a ladder built into the trunk of the tree. The wood is stained so dark it is almost black, and it's too perfect for words.

Sylvia would love it. After Mina reactivated my phone, I discovered several concerned messages from her. I had used her address and bank statements kept arriving; she wanted to know that I was alright. It was good to talk to her, to tell her I was okay.

The porch of the tree house is too small to sleep on, but if Sylvia were here, she'd find a way. When I spent the night at her house, I never asked her if I would find my way one day. Even if she told me yes, I never would have believed her.

"You built me a tree house?" Tears collect in the corner of my eyes, and not from the wind that cuts like a knife.

Nolan lets go of my hand, scratching his fingers through the beard he's grown. "It seemed like something you would like." He stomps a collection of dead leaves at our feet, and then he pulls something out of his pocket, dangling a key from his pinched-together fingers. "You never had a place of your own, and I decided it was about time you had something that was entirely yours." He juts his chin in the direction of the tree house. "I'll only enter if I'm invited."

Nolan takes my hand, turns it over, and places the key in my palm. I stare at it before closing my fist over the metal, feeling the ridges press into my skin. Before I can even understand what I'm feeling, Nolan says, "Go take a look."

He waits for me to put a foot onto the ladder, which I eventually do and climb up to the small deck surrounding the house. I might as well have wings because I am a bird up here. My hand shakes when I unlock my front door, and that's when I start crying. *My front door.* This shouldn't be what gets me emotional, but it is, and I swipe my goat-hair-covered sleeve across my eyes, stepping inside.

An old leather wingback chair sits next to an end table that I'm pretty sure Nolan built. A vase sits atop the table, filled with branches that still have a few golden leaves clinging to the stems. If I touched them, they would turn to dust. There's a small circular rag rug in front of the chair, and that's it. I spin a circle in the room and find one more detail. Right next to the door is a framed picture of Nolan and me.

When we arrived at Jay's a few months ago, Nolan stopped his truck right before we pulled onto his property. We got out and stood on the gravel road, then Nolan pulled me close and took our picture. *To whatever comes next,* he whispered in my ear.

I press my finger to the glass above our faces, leaving the smudge of my fingerprint that I'll have to clean later. Then sit in the chair in my very own house. In Tinlee Bay I had my own apartment for about five seconds, and as much as I loved it, it was never meant to be mine. Here we all share Jay's house; Jay has the master, I have the guest bedroom, and Nolan has the pull-out couch.

I don't know how long we'll stay here. Planning ahead is not something I do. Time has always been sectioned off in digestible units. Today. Tomorrow. Maybe next week, but never forever. Forever was a mythical unicorn that did not exist in my world. I was wrong about a lot of things, and now I understand that forever is standing outside in the bitter cold waiting for me to invite him in.

Taking a breath to slow my racing heart, I tug my phone out of my pocket.

I swear it doesn't even ring before Nolan answers. "Hey."

I have to swallow before I can talk. "Hey, yourself." I walk to the front door, stopping in front of the picture Nolan took. *Whatever comes next,* and I know the answer.

I take another breath. "I was wondering. If you're not busy right now, would you like to come over to my house?"

Nolan doesn't answer. His feet scrape against the wood as he climbs the ladder, and then there's a knock on the door.

Tapping the red circle on the screen of my phone, I twist the door knob.

Nolan steps into the house he built for me, wrapping me in his arms, and leading me to the only chair in the room. He sits, gently pulling me onto his lap, but I wriggle out of his arms.

"I'll crush you."

Nolan sighs. "Would you stop saying that?"

This is another conversation we've had multiple times. I'm still not used to him loving all of me, but I'm trying. I bite my cheek, then smile. His arms envelop me the moment I sit back down.

"I know you're nervous about the trip, but it's going to be great, I promise." Leaning my head against his shoulder, I nod. "And then," he says, winding a finger around the end of my hair, "we'll come home."

When you spend your life in the foster system, the words *forever* and *home* are golden tickets tucked inside chocolate bars. The likelihood you'll ever find one isn't promising, but there's always a flare of hope that when the next door opens maybe it will work out. And then one day you stop hoping altogether because following the tail of that comet burning through the sky of your desire is too painful.

So *forever* and *home* become words that lose all defined edges; they become meaningless because they've never been real.

Forever is a lifetime but it can also be a heartbeat, and mine is thudding against my ribs. I lift my face from the warmth of Nolan's shoulder. I'm still not sure how my heart found his, but I am thankful. Inching my face closer to Nolan's, I kiss him for what could be a heartbeat or a lifetime because this forever home is all mine.

Acknowledgments

It really does take a village to raise a book.

Rachel May, thank you is such a small phrase but I mean it with my entire heart. I could not imagine a better brain-gymnastics coach than you. One day I'm going to cash in on all the hugs I owe you.

Jennie Wexler, you told me *writing is the reward*, and I think about that often. It has served as a guidepost on this wild journey. Thank you.

Lindsey Ray Redd, you are a cheerleader, a champion of stories, and a gift to my heart. I love the books you write and need more of them of my shelf.

Barbara Kloss, you kept me sane, made me laugh, and helped me believe that I could do this.

Bethany, Clara, Jennifer, Katie, Lou, Shayna, and Sommer, you are the dream team of beta readers. Thank you for giving me your time and feedback. I appreciate each of you so much.

Sophie, having you as a critique partner has made my stories better. You are thoughtful, encouraging, and I'm thankful for your friendship across the miles.

Molly, what a blessing you are to me, your friendship is

such a gift. I am thankful for your keen observations as you read my pages, and the emojis you leave in the comments.

My editors, Micheline Ryckman, Deborah O'Carroll, and Alicia Whitaker, thank you for knowing where all the commas are supposed to go.

Kate, you are the best big sister I could ask for. Thank you for reading early pages and praying for me every step of the way.

Mom and Dad, thank you for encouraging me to keep going, and not just with my writing. When I wanted to drop out of school in first grade you didn't let me and that was for the best. I love you.

Zachary, Declan, and Imani, being your mom is the most spectacular privilege of my life. I love you past the wild winds and back again.

David, life has not always been easy but I am thankful for your love and the way your follow Jesus. You are the rectangle to my squiggle.

My living hope Jesus Christ, I would be lost without you. Thank you for saving me and writing your story across my heart.

About the Author

Hannah Stone is a poet and award-winning author who writes stories that wrap around your heart. She lives in the Pacific Northwest, where she shuttles kids to activities while dreaming up her next novel.

Connect with her at hannahstonewrites.com or on Instagram @hannahstonewrites.